T0103540

IT'S OK
TO FALL IN
Love
AGAIN

DEVI RAGHUVANSHI

IT'S OK
TO FALL IN
Love
AGAIN

PARTRIDGE

Print information available on the last page.

To order additional copies of this book, contact
Partridge India
000 800 10062 62
orders.india@partridgepublishing.com

www.partridgepublishing.com/india

ACKNOWLEDGEMENTS

I acknowledge and express my gratitude to my wife SUSHMA, for the input, spell check and all the inspiration and ideas, I conceived watching the degree of her patience.

My elder daughter PREETI deserves special mention for the emotional and financial support in bringing out the publication of this book.

I would like PAYAL, my younger daughter to be a partner in my this endeavour. Frankly speaking I have copied some of her blogs to make my book rich and true.

Finally I thank all my friends on Facebook, my college mates, for encouraging me to write this book. My heartfelt thanks, will not be complete unless I mentioned the big help I got from "Bhagvad Gita' and 'Google', the boss for anything.

You all are part of my these efforts BIG or SMALL.

DECLARATION

The contents of this book are wild imaginations of the author. Any resemblance of names, places or incidences are purely coincidental and unintentional.

The author does not take any responsibility for the loss or damages to anyone on account of publication of this book except he expresses his regrets for the damages if any.

CONTENTS

DEDICATION

Dedicated to my Parents, who made me to read and write, while they were just the farmers.

CHAPTER – 1

Flashback

It was still dawn when Ravi stepped out of the cab and walked towards the entry gate of Delhi Airport. The early morning February air was pleasantly cold.

Ravi was travelling to Mumbai to attend a college friend's wedding. It has been 17 years since they graduated from the same college. This wedding was going to be reunion of their batchmates. But what he didn't know, was that the reunion would begin with much ahead of time right in the queue in front of the airline check-in counter.

Ravi was almost sure it was she – same height, same long hair, same complexion. Curiosity had his eyes glued to her. And then about 60 seconds later when she turned, she proved him right. His ex-girlfriend stood two places ahead of him in that queue. They have met only once after the college farewell.

She turned and came face to face with him. Yes, she was Kavya. The first eye contacts, made them wanted to meet.

Ravi – Hi, Kavya, it's quite some time, we met. How are you?
Kavya – I am good Ravi, how are you and where off to?

They both univocally said, Ajay's marriage and the reunion. Their destination was same, aim was one but they were two different people sitting on a coffee table in airport lounge, they started knowing each other once again after a gap of so many years.

Ravi – I am working for Microsoft and based in U.S. I did my Master's degree from U.S. immediately after my B.E./M.E. and joined this company. Beyond this he did not elaborate anything about himself and the family.

Kavya – I am working for DLF Gurgaon since last so many years, immediately after my graduation and I am now staying with my parents in NOIDA. History started unfolding and the clouds of their past started scattering and Ravi went in the past. May be, Kavya also was lost in the thoughts of their early life and subsequent sequence of events.

CHAPTER – 2

The Story Begins

R avi was born in some distant unknown western U.P. village where to follow the law of land, was limited only in the books to pass your primary and secondary educational exams and beyond this, it was only the law of head of the family and a group of elders with same set of minds, and thinking and were not prepared to think logics. For them laws were written, accepted and defined and were, may be 200 or more years old. Though Ravi's father Veer Singh was a head master in a nearby village and was the most qualified and educated person with a B.A. B.Ed. degree but his intellectual environment and vision were limited not so see beyond those approx. 40 odd villages and their inhabitants. The only additional qualification or expertise he had, was that, he only could read and write URDU language and Ravi remembers that most of the Muslims staying in his village used to come to him to get their letters read and to know the contents.

Pooja was also born and brought up in a similar family of teachers with the same attitude, temperament and same thoughts. The birth of a girl child in the family was considered as a curse to the family. It is because of this unpious and unorthodox thinking in the entire area and surrounding states that the male, female ratio, over there, came to be 1000 to 850-875. Pooja was daughter of Karan Pal, a primary teacher and was from a neighbouring village, 5 miles away than that of Ravi's village.

It rained in plenty one year, crops boomed and financial status of both the families improved considerably. More than the mercy of rains, wise sense prevailed in the minds of Karan Pal and Veer Singh that they both sent their kids to schools. Their basic education started together in their schools. Ravi was four and half years and Pooja was four years and two months.

They both started as toddlers and were growing fast. Soon they reached 9th standard. The school, in Pooja's village was only upto 8th standard so in 9th class she was shifted to high school in Ravi's village and they became classmates from 9th standard. Pooja's uncle used to drop and pick her up from school. As the kids grew up a little more, their innocence started waning and their acts of mischief started appearing. Though they were just reaching adolescence, but they were ignorant of the physical and mental changes in them. So far, they were not differentiating between them as male and female. Till now, they were just a boy and a girl.

Adolescence is an important time for the development of brains, skill and this emotional development was happening at their own speed. Changes in the teenage brain, affect the child's behavior. This change of body and mind is clearly visible in girls like breast development and menstruation starts, where in boys changes in voice, growth of body and facial hair, erection and ejaculation take place rapidly. Though Pooja and Ravi were aware of these changes in them but they were hesitant in admitting and acknowledging them. They pretended to be innocents as usual.

Ravi and Pooja were growing and time was moving faster than them. They both reached in 10th standard which was a board examination and the result of 10th class decides the future of the students whether they will pursue engineering, medicines, accounts or administration. Special residential classes were arranged for all the students, both boys and girls for 3 months before their final examinations. They were put in two classrooms like a common hostel under the supervision and care of P.T. teacher Komal Singh.

Ravi and Pooja were not in love as they hardly knew the meaning of it but they certainly had a strong liking for each other. It may be of infatuation or puppy love but they were together most of the time knowingly or unknowingly. Since they were kids of two school teachers known to each other nicely so the friendly togetherness was not considered as some thing which should not have been there.

CHAPTER – 3

Ravi & Pooja in 10ᵗʰ Standard

Their relationship at this stage can be defined on their behavioural attitudes like "Today Ravi will not go home for lunch as Pooja has brought her lunch box and the other day she will go to his place as she has not brought the lunch box." Ravi's mother Anjali was used to such situations and she had a special liking for Pooja with no future wild imaginations as they were never possible for local customs, rituals and laws made by the elders some 200 years back.

Similarly in their night classes, after the study they both used to sleep in that hostel type arrangements.

Ravi would always sleep without covering himself as he knew that Pooja will wake up sometimes in the middle of night and cover him with a bed sheet. Now Ravi has made this as his habit knowingly and Pooja would do it religiously everyday. He would purposely forget to bring his sweater and Pooja would give him one of her's. He would remain shivering till she made him comfortable.

This attraction was growing between them by leaps and bounds and they were to themselves without any worry of the world around. To their luck, even Komal Singh, the warden so called, was also very casual in discharging his duties and this duo escaped his eyes for a little intimate moments of exchanging sweaters and Pooja covering Ravi with a bed sheet in the middle of the night.

CHAPTER – 4

Veer Singh's Farm House

Years back, almost all the affluent farmers were having a four walled structure with few rooms to store cattle feed and large open enclosure to keep their herd safe. The same thing, now a days is called farm houses or second homes. Veer Singh had a similar place one mile away from his house and he had many buffaloes and cows and a tractor for cultivation.

Veer Singh used to go to his second house everyday after coming back from his school and looked after his agriculture and animals. He had a large following in his village and the adjoining villages. He had a clout so at times, he used to run a parallel court and decide, minor disputes and used to part the big decisions to the local Panchayats.

Karan Pal was a strong supporter of Veer Singh for two reasons, one they were both teachers and second they were from the same caste. In addition to this, their kids were studying together in same class and same school. They used to meet too frequently and used to have lunch or dinner either at Ravi's or Pooja's places. Few people were even jealous of their solid friendship.

Everything was falling in place and they did not imagine what is stored in their destiny in times to come.

CHAPTER – 5

Ravi and Pooja As Adolescents

The transition from Adolescence to teenage period is a very exciting phase of life and the kids, specially school students want to experiment and explore the unknown world of sexuality and in absence of or lack of adequate knowledge, they indulge in this experimental type of sexual activity.

Ravi and Pooja did not know much about male and female relationship but the anxiety and inquisitiveness drove them to understand each other as to why there is a special bond between them. If may not be only friendship as they both have so many friends but it doesn't matter if any one of their friends does not come to school or remain unmet for days together. It is only Ravi for Pooja, or Pooja for Ravi, this happens. Why Ravi wants to touch her every time or why Pooja doesn't feel awkward when Ravi touches her? Big question for little brains but they are not that little now.

During these teen years of Ravi and Pooja, they both started feeling the effect of hormonal and physical changes like puberty. They started noticing an increase in sexual feelings. Sexual orientation was like an emotional, romantic inclination towards each other. Ravi used to find himself in sexual thoughts and attraction towards Pooja and his these thoughts were intense. He had experienced love of parents, brothers, sisters and friends but this feeling of love with Pooja was different. His love to Pooja had three ingredients;

1) Attraction........ the desire to kiss and hold her hand
2) Closeness........ the bond of sharing everything including thoughts, feelings and secrets
3) Commitment.... An unwritten promise to oneself to stick to her through ups and downs of relationship

He was still trying to find out whether the attraction without closeness is more like a crush or infatuation or it was a romantic love, attraction with closeness.

Ravi did not understand it much until he saw his uncle in act with his wife and understood that something like this happens and he thought to himself that he must explore it. Till now, he only learnt from his friends and seniors in school. He started searching the opportunities and the place. Pooja all along was not aware of Ravi's mental status except she understood that his looking at Pooja, now was conspicuously missing that innocence. They now seemed to be demanding something from me and I enjoyed his these roving eyes. Puppy love was slowly maturing in both of them.

"What does she think of this?"

"She didn't clearly conclude as what exactly is going on in their minds. The charisma of Ravi is always standing in front of her mind and it appears that they both are deviating from their path of studies." She decided to talk to Ravi and sort out.

CHAPTER – 6

Khap Rules

As discussed in Chapter-2, it is imperative to understand the background of area where the youth of both these kids was blossoming. This region of western U.P. was same as existed in Haryana, Rajasthan, M.P. where everything was happening based on those draconian laws of 200 years. The entire society was under Patriarchal system and the head of the family or group of people were acting at despots. In some areas, it was known as Khap Panchayats.

There was certain rules which were not existing in Indian constitution. Like in Khap Panchayats regime, sometimes marriages are performed by pressurizing one or both the parties without their free will and free consent. This is carried out through coercion, fear, abduction, threat inducement and deception. Khap Panchayats prohibit Sagotra and inter-caste marriage.

Marriage within same gotras is forbidden since in that case a boy and a girl are regarded as brother and sister (INCEST).

Marraiges in different gotras are forbidden if a boy and girl belong to same village or physically adjoining villages.

Inter-caste marriages are strictly barred and the Khap Panchayats are asking for amendment of Hindu Marriage Act 1955. These Panchayats think that they are above Indian Law in western U.P. and Haryana.

Any violation of the Khap laws invites punishment similar to Taliban. At times it may be decapitation and social bycott. Any couple marrying beyond these defined rules, can also be subjected to be executed and their bodies being hung on trees as a lesson for others not to break the laws. These people are so united that the affected people do not resort to Indian Constitutional laws.

CHAPTER – 7

Ravi & Pooja in 12ᵗʰ Standard

Both Ravi and Pooja decided that now was the time to concentrate on studies as the board examination of 10ᵗʰ Standard were at a stone's throw and they both studied hard and harder and did at least revisions of all the subjects four times. They also completed solutions of last 5 years examination papers. Since hard work never fails, they both passed their board examination securing first class with distinction in Maths, Science and English.

As the results were encouraging, both Veer Singh and Karan Pal thought of admitting them in Inter Science in Govt. Intermediate college, Meerut. Ravi stayed in the hostel while Pooja stayed with one of his uncle's family. As the destiny decided, they again started living together in and after college hours. They both used to go to their villages together on weekends and used to come back on all Mondays. Two years passed and they were both in 12ᵗʰ Standard, few months away again from their final board examination, the result of which was to decide their future line up of career. Pooja's parents were of the view that once, she passes 12ᵗʰ Standard, they might stop her education and get her married. There was an unwritten diktat from so called Khap Panchayat that marry the girls at early age to avoid rapes. This did not go very well with Veer Pal and he advised Karan Pal that let Pooja continue studies. She is a brilliant girl, she might become an Engineer, Doctor or IAS officer. Let her pursue her career and provide her opportunities which you and me, were deprived off. This was the happiest and proudest moment for Karan Pal and Ravi was more than happy to hear this. He thought to himself that Pooja will be more available to him even if they choose a different lines of professional education. They both again lost in their books. They followed the same pattern of combined studies. Picked up last 10 years question papers and solved them and this made their base of examination solid. They also took help of you-tube lectures of their subjects and found out that the contents of you-tube material was more conclusive as compared to the contents of conventional books.

It was not true that they were, all the time busy in books. They also had some time to refresh their minds and to remove the fatique of studies by going out for tea, snacks and also satisfying their limited urge of kissing and hugging. Pooja never felt bad on his these minor adult habits. He used to tell Pooja that whenever I see deep into your magic eyes, something starts happening to me and all I want on those moments, is kissing you and kissing you. Pooja very coolly used to explain to him that we must decide our priorities first. All this can wait. Ok, Pooja said Ravi and they restarted their first priority. They both did well in their final year 12th Standard examination and stood first and 3rd in their college and got their names written on a blackboard, called Role of honours.

They both were advised further by the college counselors as to which line, they had to choose and also advised to appear for CET (Combined Entrance Test) for admission in Engineering, Architecture, Medicine etc. courses and the relevant colleges. Ravi was interested to go for Engineering and Pooja had a choice of Architecture over Engineering. They both appeared in the CET and passed the entrance examination. Ravi got a choice in IIT Mumbai whereas Pooja got admission in Delhi college of Architecture.

Both were happy and the happiest people were the parents of both the kids. They were more proud than being happy because both Ravi and Pooja were becoming the first people in the entire region to become first Engineer and first Architect. For the first time, both Veer Singh and Karan Pal celebrated their this success on drinks at Veer Singh's second home called Farm House. Ravi and Pooja were both on cloud 9 but deep inside their hearts they also had a feeling of pain that they would be away from each other for a period of minimum 5 years as Architecture was 5 years course. The feeling of unfulfillness, gave Ravi a feeling to meet Pooja and explore her bodily love for him. Pooja was more patient with him but she could not resist Ravi's advances.

CHAPTER – 8

Ravi & Pooja before next colleges

There was certain eyes in the society who were vigilantly following both Ravi and Pooja. Since they were together, most of the time, their this togetherness was being viewed as illegitimate relationship. Frankly speaking, the same people were jealous of them. Both Ravi and Pooja tried their best to keep their relationship under wraps but as people say that ISHQ and MUSK (Love and Scent) do not remain unnoticed for a long time.

One day both of them were caught in a compromising position in a sugarcane field. They were so engrossed in the act that they did not even know that they are targeted and being caught by local people. Then the hell broke loose. The news spread like wild fire. Soon everybody in the village and surrounding villages came to know about this and this union of Ravi and Pooja, became a point of discussion in all corners, all houses in that entire region. Some disgruntled and jealous people gave Pooja a name of slut and whore. The poor thing was not in position to move out of her house and similarly the most affected people, were the parents of both Ravi and Pooja.

CHAPTER – 9

Justice or Injustice begins

The unauthorized court called Khap Panchayat with almost 90 percent uneducated age old men held their first meeting to decide on what punishment is to be awarded to Ravi and Pooja and the two families. One set of smoking tobacco machine called Hukka, was arranged for them as this tobacco only will bring the facts out of that biggest crime, love which these kids committed.

Without even discussing the episode, without even asking Ravi and Pooja, without even asking the witnesses, it was pronounced that it was a rape. There was no full stop to the outrageous diktats of these Khap leaders. The Panchayat asked both Ravi and Pooja to tie a Rakhi and live like brother and sister. They also ruled that there existed a Bhaichara (kind of blood relationship) between two families so they cannot marry. This was answered when Ravi told them his resolute to marry Pooja. Living under extreme pressure from villagers, following the Khap's order the hapless and helpless couple had no option but to retaliate and leave the village if necessary.

This further infuriated the judges. Both the families of Veer Siingh and Karan Pal were humiliated and threatened with a social boycott. The Panchayat also directed both the parents to disown their kids from all properly, belongings and land and also a fine of Rupees Two Lacs each. Both the parents opposed the Khap Panchayat's decision but they had to bow down against the majority judgement of the Panchayat.

The Panchayat further directed that in event of non-compliance of the orders, the couple will be subjected to murder and hang their bodies to a tree so it becomes an exemplary punishment for others not to commit such crime. Ravi protested and refused obedience. He only said yes I am responsible for the incidence. I will marry Pooja and move out of this region called Taliban. Declaring punishment on our parents is against law of the land and I am not accepting your verdict. Do whatever you all want to do. Gone are the days when you used to impose your own laws.

I know that over the years, Khap Panchayat, belonging to this belt of western U.P., Haryana, Rajasthan and M.P. states, have earned a lot of hate with their ridiculous diktats and rules on love, love marriages or women issues but no positive action has been taken against you people or against these draconian rules out of fear of loosing vote banks. I will fight against these traditions. Some youth supported Ravi but the support was far too less and far to achieve.

CHAPTER – 10

Families uprooted

Throughout this ordeal, Veer Singh stood like a rock with Karan Pal. He told him we would marry our kids what may come but Karan Pal couldn't bear the taunts by neighbours, relations and everybody blamed Pooja calling her names. He finally decided to send Pooja to Canada. Karan Pal's brother-in-law was based in Vancouver. He also wanted his daughter to be away from Ravi. Pooja met Ravi and explained to him that she had no option but to leave him and the country.

Ravi told Pooja to have a little patience. "We would fight these people. In case, we fail, I will not let you die in front of me. In worst case, I will ask you to pick up some clothes and all your documents, certificates. I know that we have to struggle and start a fresh. The road ahead is very thorny, scary and it is like crossing seven seas on a fishing boat all alone. The task is tough and destiny is uncertain but yes, I will somehow see you as an architect and for that whatever has to be done, I will do it even at the cost of leaving IIT Mumbai."

Pooja was more matured and replied, "Ravi I do not have an iota of disbelief that you will not do all this to me but we are still young and this world is so cruel. Let me go to Canada and you complete your engineering, we will meet, God willing for sure. Please do not carry any guilt in your mind because whatever happened, the other day, we both were responsible and I have now become more confident on you that you can fight evils and stand on your feet." My mama is in the process of making documents for me to travel to Canada on a student's VISA and this might take another 15/20 days. Be strong, do not deviate from your goal. I loved you as a kid, as an adult and I would respect our this relationship for times to come. I suggest that you also stop fighting this system as this evil is centuries old. I would meet you in sometime.

Ravi could do nothing except crying or spilt milk. I do not know anything now Pooja what I am going to do and what's going to happen to me but I would remember your last words and these words, would be my inspiration. I would take care of your family the way you would have done. Pooja left him and this was his last meeting with Ravi before she flew to Canada after a fortnight.

Over here, the burden of humiliation, hearing the names like slut and whore for his darling daughter, made Karan Pal and his wife mentally sick and their health started deteriorating day by day. Both developed high degree of B.P. and Diabetes. They entered a bad phase of depression. Even Veer Singh could not help them to come to terms. They used to become violent after seeing Ravi as in their mind, Ravi was responsible for everything bad in their life including the Pooja episode. Finally they couldn't stand the cruelty of this world and both Karan Pal and his wife committed suicide by consuming pesticides. This left Pooja, Ravi and everyone shattered. Even the Khap felt guilty and bad but nothing could be done. Pooja vowed never to return to her village.

As life goes on and time doesn't wait for anybody, Pooja, a rebellion concentrated on her studies in Canada.

Ravi and Veer Singh also could not bear the loss of his friend Karan Pal. They too sold their land and belongings and left their village once forever and settled in Bhiwani, Haryana. Ravi on advice from his parents and his commitment to Pooja withdrew from fighting that Khap Panchayat and joined IIT Mumbai in Civil Engineering Ist B.Tech (C).

The two families scattered but feeling of being together united once again. Veer Singh promised himself that he will take care of Pooja as his daughter and future daughter-in-law. Ravi with a guilt of killing a family, moved on in life and his sole aim was to see Pooja happy in all circumstances.

CHAPTER – 11

Ravi leaves the village

The very thought that Pooja is not with him, which was a reality, sent shock waves in his spine and his entire physical and mental status was shaken and crippled. He wanted to get out of the patriarchal society immediately. When he was separated from Pooja, it was the hardest decision, he has ever made in his life by letting Pooja go. He felt that the whole world was shattering in front of his eyes and he could do nothing to stop it happen. It affected him physically, emotionally and mentally.

During this process, he was going through family crisis and then to college stress. And for Pooja, the story was no different. The whole separation affected her more than Ravi thought. She had the worst experience of life as she lost her family, Ravi whom she truly loved. All, she did was cry, cry and only cry and could not sleep at all.

Ravi was at the verge of breakdown but soon, he remembered the words, Pooja told him before leaving for Canada. Her these words were working as a strength to survive. She said, "There is always another chance for everything but fact is, there is no chance of another life so dream it, live it and love it."

With a very heavy heart, a mistake in his mind and dastardly act of the Panchayat and its subsequent loss of lives, loss of name and fame. Ravi left his village to Bhiwani and then to Mumbai.

It was painful to part with his friends, parents, relatives whom he was once the dearest person on earth. What mistake he committed? He simply loved Pooja and wanted her to be a partner in journey of his life. He in any case was not going to stay in that environment for a long time. In fact he didn't belong to those conditions, cultural and social rules, set by that patriarchal society some 200 years back.

What more, he was missing in his village significantly, was listening to the chirping of bulbuls, parakeets and sound of gurgling water from his tube-well. He was going to miss that wonderful view of 'sarson ke khet' and the sunset behind his golden fields. He was never going to be part of that friendly farmers gathering again. Some friends wanted to pack him some 'sarson ka saag' to take with him but to take it where? was a question in his mind. He could never forget the beauty and fragrance of his sugarcane fields where he had spent a good time of his childhood and youth including some adulterous acts, he had performed with Pooja without understanding, the consequences of these acts on separation. Similarly the tuar daal fields which were very exotic and dense and provided much needed privacy to the young couples including Ravi and Pooja. All this was looking like a wild dream and all the incidences of his life, so far were moving one by one in front of his eyes.

He left the villages with so many wet eyes but yes, he definitely sowed the seed of revolt in the youth to overtake all old draconian laws.

CHAPTER – 12

Ravi at IIT Mumbai & Pooja in Canada

Ravi joined IIT Mumbai and became a hosteller in the campus. The institute is one of the premier institutes in technology and management programmes. It's an old institute for graduates but for Masters and MBAs, it was further extended in the year 1995 and serves the objective of transforming professionals with technology background into leaders of tomorrow. Life at IIT-B is an amalgamation of fun and duties. While the classes and assignments manage to keep students busy during mornings and late nights respectively. The rest of the day allows them to pursue their own interests. Some of them find the peace in playing cricket and football in the hostel grounds while some of them head to the student activity centre to play badminton or go for a swim.

The best thing about the campus is the campus itself with lush green shade of trees and lawns. There is a magnetism about this institute including brand value. Apart from the subject combinations, there is something about the coveted institute that it attracts so many students. Friends, parties, gossiping, hostels, assignments, fun competitions, sports, rains, seniors, lingo, mentors, sleeping during lectures, sleeping late nights.......... This is all about IIT-B, what do you call a girl in IIT-B .... VISITOR, poor joke but it is true. There is a shortage of girls. People are mad about girls rather desperate about them. Most of the people think that life at IIT-B is stressful. No, an average day goes with 2-3 hours of study. Most of the students study just a day before exams. They watch movies, T.V. shows and can be found online on Facebook or Whatsapp. Ravi who lost interest in all these activities remained with catching up with some sleep and nothing attracted him except studies.

The distance was not a fun but it was a pain for both of them. Ravi and Pooja couldn't stop loving each other just because they were living too far away. Pooja was unable to concentrate in college. The very long time separation from Ravi, led her to increased anxiety and depression. Pooja after few weeks of entering in Architecture course in Canada, started feeling the pain of being alone in a big family of his maternal uncle Rajendra Singh. She started feeling guilty for the loss of her parents. For everything, she started thinking that she is responsible. Soon she entered in a phase of depression. She became irritated and angry on petty issues. She had a continuous feeling of sadness and hopelessness. She also lost interest in socializing, lost appetite. Some changes in her sleep pattern, were also noticed. She was not concentrating on anything including her college activities. She was always looking tired and fatigued.

When her uncle noticed all these changes, she was taken for medical treatment where different medications like acupuncture, yoga, meditation were given along with different medicines and anti depressants yoga exercises.

This treatment definitely helped Pooja to recover fast but the main reason for improvement was due to Pooja attending spiritual discourses conducted by ISKCON, international society for Krishna consciousness. She also started reading Bhagwad Gita. The healing process started and she followed the advice of Gita.

There was a race against time, Ravi passed first three semesters and was preparing for 4th semester examination. First two semesters were more or less what he studied in his 12th standard except the engineering drawing. 3rd semester was having subjects related with his Civil Engineering. Ravi had a girl, his batch mate, his partner in Engineering survey of ground. She was helping Ravi in taking the ground measurement by using theodolite and other engineering equipments to know the contours of the ground and in soil testing laboratory. This was always like a joint effort or combined studies. Their assignments, practicals and sessionals were common so they had lot of opportunity to be together in college and otherwise.

Ravi knew this girl Kavya for around 18 months now. She was the most charismatic, enthusiastic, outspoken, adventurous girl who was living and loving life in every single moment. Ravi by virtue of circumastances hurting and hunting past, was completely opposite, shy, studious, afraid of exploring new avenues of life or in short afraid of coming out of his shell. This doesn't mean that he never appreciated Kavya for her work and sometimes even her appearance or her dresses. His only problem was that he would not speak unless coerced or provoked. Kavya was aware of his this attitude and she wanted to understand his nerves but most of the time, it was like finding a needle in the haystack. But she never lost hopes. She continued striving for unfolding the mystery of his silence.

Over there in Canada, Pooja was provided with a basic education for a future in the profession. Her college, School of Architecture, Vancouver, University of British Columbia, started providing her an extraordinary foundation related with design field. This college was affiliated with National Capital Region Canada, Mortgage and Housing Corporation, Natural Art Centre, Aviation Science and Technology career. She also obtained expertise in Landscape Architecture.

CHAPTER – 13

Fortune/Misfortune strikes Pooja

For Pooja, the time moved on lightening speed or knee jerk speed. Too many things happened for her in too small a span. When Pooja had a nervous decline and was admitted under medical care, it was diagnosed that she is two months pregnant. When this was communicated to her, hell broke down on her and on her immediate family. Both her maternal uncle and aunty took it as another accident of life and decided to find a solution for Pooja on permanent basis. The first option considered by them, was to get the pregnancy terminated, second being marry Pooja with someone without informing someone or third being that let Pooja deliver the baby at a place for away from Vancouver where they all lived.

It was more or less a teenage pregnancy. Pooja thought to herself that there was no point discussing as she knew that it was a weak moment that has led to such a stage. She was troubled herself and was scribbling some letter which was disturbing her and the family. All the time, she was lost in thoughts like the social stigma, associated with being unwed mother was so much that it might lead her to commit suicide because in our society, pregnancy outside marriage was considered a humiliation that would affect not only her but also her family. Such a woman is ostracized in most of the societies in India and abroad. The immediate family and extended family which should provide social protection to the mother, leave her alone considering her a social and financial burden.

She also knew that a single woman, both at home, college or at work, has to face many advances from men young and old, married and unmarried. To be single and specially an unwed mother, is taken as that she is available or easy to gain access to. Further more, what is more critical is that the responsibility of a child born outside marriage rests solely on mother.

With so many adversities in front of Pooja, there was a silver lining for her. She had the best of support from Rajendra Singh and family. They were overprotective for Pooja and were ready to accept any of the three options which Pooja approves. Secondly the social and cultural stigma was less as compared to Indian situations. In Canada, there were so many unwed mothers due to those weak moments or due to live in relationships. Thirdly, the college management accepted her request of missing one semester and appearing after Pooja's delivery.

Pooja at no point of time, was prepared to get her pregnancy terminated, come what may and take total charge of the situation. Rajendra Singh wanted to seek Pooja's approval to let Ravi know about Pooja's this state of affairs. He asked her whether to call Ravi here to meet you Pooja. Pooja said, No. He had his set of problems, once informed, he would leave everything including his college and her dream of seeing him as professional engineer, will be shattered. I will not let him know anything. Time will heal his wounds and mine too. What would you tell your kid when he or she would ask you the name of the father. I would decide what the situation would warrant. If required, I would tell them the truth and Mama, let us cross the bridge when it comes to. Her voice was firm and defiant.

Pooja decided not to abort her child not because she still loved Ravi but because she should give her child a right to live and prove himself/ herself that she doesn't care about the society now. This so called society was never there when she was in depression or for any of her needs. Only her maternal uncle and aunty were standing behind her like a solid rock. She also decided against going back to Ravi again. She stood up on her own feet.

Time doesn't wait for anything or anybody. Pooja cleared her first semester of first year of Architecture, missed the second semester. Pooja delivered twins, two healthy babies one son and one daughter, five minutes younger to her brother. Rajendra Singh, his wife named two babies after consulting Pooja and they were named as Samar (Sam) [A mix of Pooja and Ravi] and Simaran (Sim) [A mix of Pooja and Ravi again].

Pooja for the first time after such a long turmoil in life, felt immensely happy and full of life. She also became matured before the age and circumstances made her a mother before even she became a woman. She started her journey of a complete woman and the mother of substance. Pooja had become now a woman of substance. She has faced so many challenges in life with dignity and grace and was able to avenge the insults to her. Though she was basically a very religious woman but no Krishna came to her rescue.

CHAPTER – 14

Ravi & Kavya in 4th Semester

When you are part of an organization, be it be college, office, it is impossible to function alone without any relationship back up. It is not necessary that all relationships will be fuelled by work infused motive but eventually they land up in some lifelong friendship. For example, the members of your team work with you at very close quarters and they all play an important and significant role in your life to accomplish your goals. Some develop the most intimate relationship like you visit their homes, know each other's families and friends and even go out on short trips and holidays.

This was the relationship between Ravi and Kavya. Kavya by nature was very exuberant so she expected the entire world around her to be lively and cheerful. They were both preparing for their 4th semester examinations. With time, they both started liking each other. As the time was limited, pressure harse, Ravi had his own sort of problems so they both focused on studies but Ravi's stoical silence was always bothering her. As she couldn't take the continuous pressure of Ravi being so apathetic, she decided to meet Ravi in between the preparatory vacations and requested him to join her for a cup of coffee in a coffee shop CCD outside their campus. Ravi reached one hour before the schedule time. He had no explanation to offer as to why he carried a nice bouquet of Orchid flowers. Kavya came on dot. She was wearing a simple Salwar Kameez but was looking stunningly beautiful. She had an innocent face. Her face had full radiance and her sparking eyes showed a high degree of confidence as if today she is going to conquer Mount Everest. A chill ran through Ravi's spine as he was full of mixed emotions and was extremely excited to see and meet her. Ravi looked at her face, she was still her usual self, smiling. Ravi also smiled and greeted her warm, held her hand and asked her to sit next to him. She patted lightly on Ravi's shoulder and said, "Stop being a kid" when she noticed that Ravi was smiling even when his pain was trying to take over.

Kavya as a very matured girl took Ravi in confidence and explained to him that life is full of ups and downs......... you fall, you hurt, you struggle and get up again. There is nothing permanent in life including your and my life. You share, you love and face each new day with courage, knowing that the best is yet to come. Ravi, please come out of your shell and live and love life like any other IITians. Though Ravi knew that there is no other way except what Kavya has told but hearing it from Kavya, gave him an extra strength for replacement of his agony rather than surrendering to it. He became acquiescent and self-resolved. He saw deep into Kavya's eyes for the first time and felt that, yes, the flame is lit and Kavya became much more than just being a project partner.

Like everyone says, "Time heals every pain including the pain of tragedy of the past. Ravi never believed this in the past because he was still experiencing the bitterness and loneliness of his past when Pooja left him. There was no alternate but to accept the reality, so he decided to overcome this problem. He now wanted to feel good despite the realities of the situation. It was very difficult for him to feel good when his heart has been broken and he has lost a friend. His aim was to wake up every day and give himself and people around him, one purposeful action. One of the most effective ways to take purposeful action every day was to help others who were in need of support. Volunteering for purposeful NGOs was another relief. He thought that he was the manager of his life. If he didn't show the spirit of leadership role, life will hit default button to take control of him.

He started meditation as a routine which showed remarkable progress in his attitude. Time passed, his efforts paid, he was able to forget his past partially and started moving forward. Pooja's image was slowly blurring. He made it a point to believe that he would not confuse his present with the past and decided to take no further action on his old memories. The sad truth was that so many people were in love and not together and so many people are together and not in love.

Of course, Kavya helped him a lot in bringing Ravi back in normal flow of life.

CHAPTER – 15

Pooja in different Roles

For Pooja, walking alone was not difficult but when she has walked a mile with someone then coming back alone was more difficult. While performing dual role of mother and student, she had actually become a igneous rock without being innocuous. Hats off to Rajendra Singh and his wife, who had a much better job than what Pooja's parents would have done. They were the parents to Sam and Sim when Pooja was in college and they were parents to Pooja when she was at home. The only thought bothering both of them, was to get Pooja settled in life as they both knew, how difficult the life for Pooja would be as a single unwed mother.

Pooja started shouldering most or all the day-to-day responsibilities for raising her children and became a prime care giver as a single parent. Though she was sharing only part of responsibilities, major being shared by the immediate family, but a sense of anxiety always remained in her mind. Being young mother was affecting her education. Teenage motherhood was making her economically dependent on her maternal uncle and aunty for all her expenses for education and all expenses for her kids. Many times, a thought swam her mind to discontinue her education and start working for her livelihood which was strongly protested by her family. They used to tell her that it was a matter of only two years after which she would be in position not only to support her but to the family also. This gave her long awaited solace and strength to continue. Luckily both the kids were healthy unlike the kids born out of teenage pregnancy.

She was more worried about her children as some doctor told her during their birth that children of teen mothers, are at higher risk of intellectual, language and socio-emotional delays. Developmental disabilities and behavioral issues are increased in children born to teen mothers. They were three years then but nothing of these sorts were noticed and they were growing like any normal Indian children in Canadian ambience. Pooja was praying everytime and was always remembering and following Bhagvad Gita verses and was a firm believer that Lord Krishna was with her all the time and blessings of her elders living or immortals were doing a good job for her.

Time was moving very fast. Pooja completed her degree course in Architecture and associated special skills and the kids moved to their second home that is Kinder Garten. For the first day of their school, she offered both of them, sweet curd, considered to be auspicious before doing anything for the first time in India. A lamp was lit, flowers put in the temple of their house and special food was prepared. This was Pooja's first achievement as a mother. She touched feet of his uncle Rajendra Singh and aunty and expressed her reverence and gratitude to both of them. Tears rolled down from three pairs of eyes.

CHAPTER – 16

Ravi comes close to Kavya

Time leapt by year by year, one year, two years. The affinity between Ravi and Kavya was increasing day after days. They were initially so parallel that it appeared that they will only meet at infinity like parallel lines, but things have changed over last two years. They continued to meet for another year and corresponded and responded at most every day, sometimes twice a day. After refusing her overtures, he was finally won over by her, untiring efforts and they became lovers now. By now Ravi had become a bit outspoken and open. He started thinking in terms of taking Kavya on his/her first date. He thought that he would not make his first date boring or with ideas of unhealthy choice such as going for a booze or wine parties. So he decided to make it too interesting and unforgettable experience. Many options came to his mind. He called up Kavya and suggested to take her to (1) Sneak into the pool (2) Take her for a coffee or ice-cream break (3) Go for cycling in and around the nearby hills (4) Go for a Karaoke night (5) Go to experience some dramas in Prithvi theater (6) last but not the least, study together and be with him.

Kavya agreed to each experience but for the first date, she preferred sneaking into the pool. They both went to pool in the campus. The water in the pool was sparkling clean, cold and blue all over. It was a small adventure bringing about a lot of good feelings. It was a wonder way to have some wonderful moments of intimacy, also to build up an adrenaline and soak up the sunlight together.

This was followed by picking up a cup of coffee in the nearby coffee shop. They both realized that this is actually one of the best and most interesting dating experience. Now the soul searching started in the hearts of both Ravi and Kavya. Kavya had the first feeling of being loved by Ravi. She said to Ravi that we would go for the rest of the dating experience periodically as suggested by Ravi. Yes, studying together would be started without any loss of time. The final exams are not too far away. Ravi, so let us concentrate on your last suggested idea of a date. Yes, said Ravi. They both started 18 hours a day. They were awake studying upto wee hours of the day and sometimes used to listen early morning birds chirping. They also visited some Karaoke nights.

Kavya was damn good, trained singer and Ravi was as bad in singing as Dharmendra was in dancing. To freshen up from hard work of studies, they also visited Prithvi Theater to see some nice dramas of Anupam Kher and Mona Singh. Their hard work paid rich dividends. They both passed their 3rd year in good percentage.

They again realized that the hard work never fails. To celebrate their success, they both went to Lonavala on bicycles and came back late evening to their hostels. A nice experience of a picnic in and around hills and greenery of the journey. Ravi on the way, just held Kavya's hand and tried to attempt his first kiss and since there was only a minor resistance from Kavya, he succeeded. They both crossed the first ladder of love. Pooja was slowly and slowly disappearing from the scene. Kavya was taking her place and nearly made a unshakable place in the heart of Ravi.

They both believed in, "Don't be a beggar of love,

> Be a donor of Love,
> Beautiful people are not always good,
> But good people are always beautiful"

Both Ravi and Kavya resumed classes in 4th year, the final year. They had only one year to go before they decide on their professional and personal career. They were both studious and serious lovers now onwards. Unspoken and undecided commitment was taking shape in their lives. After two months, election to Students Council was announced and Kavya wanted Ravi to contest this election for the post of President of Students Council. She worked day and night in canvassing and Ravi was elected President with a huge margin of votes.

This victory and constant efforts of Kavya gave him tremendous confidence and he practically came out of shell of his past. Kavya was on cloud 9 after these achievements. Their relationship was simple. She fed him straight lines and he fed her straight lines. Kavya was his partner in all his acts, best friend and his lover and probably the future mother of his would be children. They were a team both on and off the stage.

Now Ravi openly started describing Kavya, like Kavya, "you have long back hair with curls that spin down your shoulders. Your skin is that Irish Peach bloom with just a touch of makeup. What a pretty little girl you are! Kavya didn't have to be genius to understand the motive behind his description. She only said don't be a kid and don't take me round and round. Ravi very politely told Kavya that it took him almost one year to tell her how he felt about Kavya. Eventually Ravi instead of kissing her on cheeks, he kissed her lightly on lips and next moment he pressed harder and he put his arms around her. Finally it was for real. Only once, he remembered, did she pull away, "it's not right Ravi" what? asked Ravi. Your this unexpected move. She did not sound to be serious in confronting Ravi.

For the first time in four years, they were alone and wanted to spend some quality time. Though they spend many more moments alone while going to theater or while coming back to hostels, but these moments today, appeared much different, silent but with mischievous smiles and adult motives. Ravi leaned over and kissed Kavya and whispered, "I Love You, Kavya". She only said, "Me Too".

They left the tennis court after this and headed straight to lake view hotel for dinner. They had some serious discussion over the dinner. Ravi asked Kavya whether her parents are aware of our this alliance? She only replied, only my elder sister knew about. Ravi further asked, what sort of qualities, you would like to have in your future husband? ADRIB came the reply. I would like to be married to a man who is stable, a good provider and a loving father to our children. He would be strong enough, would take me now and then, not very dominating type. I am a woman enough to want to the pleasure and intimacy of it. He should be completely absorbed in himself and me. What about you Ravi, what are your specifications for your wife to be? I'd like to be married to a woman who is trustworthy, respectful, open and loving mother to our children. She would stand strong in he confidence. She would be comfortable and confident in her desire for me. She would have a passion that she gets completely absorbed in herself, me and the moment.

Kavya told Ravi that our specifications to not match. I will standby against all your needs of your body and soul but you are a Chaalu type (not trustworthy) so the system would not work. Kavya's comments were full of humour which Ravi understood and reacted by saying, "you would be my wife good, bad or ugly. He became over protective to Kavya.

The final year also leapt and they both became graduate engineers. Kavya was selected by a Real Estate Giant DLF to work in Delhi as Sales & Marketing Manager and Ravi decided to do Masters either at IIT Bombay or at some foreign university in advance structural designs. Needless to mention that these moments of success, were celebrated by both of them at Fariyas Hotel, Lonavala. This time they both united in body and soul for the first time. There was no regret but a strong desire of hope and commitment for future.

Kavya left for Delhi to take up new assignment and Ravi stayed at IIT-B for his future decisions.

CHAPTER – 17

Pooja becomes a big name

Pooja was selected by D. S. Architects, Vancouver in the campus interview. DSA in Canada, are one of the biggest name in Canada, U.S. and Singapore. They are specialized architects in field of Infra-structure projects, Town Planning and high rise buildings. Within one year, she acquired name and fame to start her own architecture firm called ASR Architects Pvt. Ltd. in a small 10ft x 10ft office.

She worked hard without understanding the difference of day and night and soon became No.1 – associate of John & John Architects. John was a renowned architect famously known as John the great all over the world for his magnificent creations of Embassies of U.S., Russia and India in Canada. ASR, soon became their system partner and all important and big jobs started coming to her through John & John. She purchased a 10,000 Sqft space in the main commercial hub of the city.

She was being called for major projects for discussions along with John so it was essentially natural for both of them to be together on many occasions.

John was 38 years and Pooja was 28 years old. He had an athletic look, fair like any Canadian, good looking and his appearance was so deceptive to say that he looked around 30 years. He was soft spoken and responsible to that extent that he would take care even small, small issue like travelling and lodging arrangements of Pooja whenever she was accompanying him for meetings etc.

Once after the first meeting, they were waiting for another client in coffee shop of Hyatt Hotel at Singapore. The flight of this client got delayed by two hours so both John and Pooja had sometime to discuss about themselves. John started by saying that Pooja, I am a self-made man. I have seen ups and downs of life very closely. My parents died when I was only six years old so I have been brought up in an orphanage run and managed by church. They were all very supportive for all my needs including studies. I did my Architecture Degree from Mexico and started as an assistant in this company and finally managed to own this. I am a single man, never married and spend 25 percent of my earnings for development of the orphanage and church which provided me the pedestal to stand. Today, they are the best church and orphanage in the entire country. In fact I stopped calling it as an orphanage because, for them, I am the peon, I am the manager, I am the cook, I am the warden and I am the father of the orphanage. Sorry, I called it orphanage.

Pooja became serious and numb upon knowing this man with big virtues and minimum needs of his own. She also wondered that there existed some man like John. Pooja asked John, Sir, what shall I order for you to eat? We still have time before the meeting. John said that he is a Vegan. Pooja never heard about Vegan. She was conversant with vegetarian and non-vegetarian meals only so the word vegan sounded a bit unusual. She couldn't resist asking John what Vegan is meant? John explained, "Vegans are more strictly vegetarians as they only eat vegetarian food and they don't use items like soap, moisturizer, creams etc. made out of animal fat. She was shell shocked to know that there existed someone like John on this earth.

Pooja couldn't decide what to tell John about her? Whether to tell him the entire calendar of her life or just the summary of it hiding some of her very very personal past? But John definitely established some confidence in her and how she trusted him, she narrated her entire history so far including Ravi and her two kids. John couldn't believe his eyes and ears and more or less went into comatose. She only said that Pooja, you are a super woman and super mom who has withstood the test of time at this young age. I have so much of respect for you and it is no sympathy because you don't deserve sympathies but accolades. Any woman under your circumstances, would have either committed suicide or would have crashed. You are a brave girl. I will pray for you in Church. I do not know with which soil you are made of? Pooja appreciated and liked his kind words and John expressed desire to meet her kids and the family back home. Pooja had serenading effect on her mental status.

CHAPTER – 18

Kavya joins DLF

Kavya joined DLF, the biggest Real Estate company of India as Assistant Manager Quality Assurance and Manager Sales & Marketing. The office was situated in Gurgaon. Gurgaon has a skyline of 1100 tall buildings with modern planning. It is situated at Delhi border. It has beautiful parks like Leisure Valley Park spread over 36 acre green land, Biodiversity botanical garden or HUDA garden. It also has an epicenter like Kingdom of Dreams and Nautanki Mehal. You can fluently deal in Hindi, English, Punjabi, Haryanavi languages. There is a unity in diversity in this city. The population of Gurgaon consist of Hindu, Muslim, Sikhs, Christian and have ample scope to worship in Temples, Mosques, Churches, Gurudwaras. Transport system from Gurgaon to Delhi and neighbouring states is very efficient. It has close to 580 hotels ranging from Rs.1000/- to Rs.50,000/- per room night and have presence of all international chains of luxury hotels.

The contribution by DLF, Kavya's company in transforming Gurgoan from an old Haryana city to Gurgaon as today is 70%. The majority of IT hubs, corporate offices beautiful residential buildings and infrastructure is due to presence of DLF in the city. Kavya also had a lovely office, centrally air-conditioned, beautiful glass façade. She had wonderful company of young engineers and technocrats. All the beautiful girls of Delhi, were present in the DLF office.

There was a nice canteen for the staff so she was comfortable from all angles of ease and comfort. She was assigned 7 buildings to control for quality and timely hand over. The work was tough but she was enjoying it thoroughly. She used to go back to Vasant Vihar after the work where she was staying with her parents who were retired from CPWD and recently shifted from NOIDA. She used to miss Ravi but used to talk to him twice a day and long chat on whatsapp in the night. They were maintaining healthy long distance relationship. Ravi took admission in M.S. (Structural Engineering) at IIT-B and was to be there for next two years. For him everything was same except his love life Kavya being in Delhi. He sometimes used to talk to himself like, "I don't know how to explain love, I fell towards my girl Kavya. It never quit on me, it never died. It just got stronger. There have been lot of mistakes in my life but I have never regretted loving her." On otherside Kavya was not that comfortable and was missing him and she used to murmur as "Lord knows how tough life can be without you Ravi. When I look back, I'm certain of this, that nothing is more powerful than love, Not money, greed, hate or passion.

Waiting for each other, two years passed. Kavya become a General Manager in DLF and Ravi completed his Masters and became B.Tech (Civil) M.S. (Structural Engineer) IIT-B.

He had an assignment from MICROSOFT, New York, a very lucrative and prosperous offer. He wanted to discuss with Kavya before he accepts and moves to New York or rejects to stay in India and explore other avenues. He wanted to meet Kavya in Delhi as early as possible. Kavya asked him to come to Delhi, meet her parents also who were now aware of their relationship.

CHAPTER – 19

Ravi goes to Delhi

Ravi asked his father Veer Singh to come to Delhi stay at Janpath Hotel at Janpath Road which has been booked by him from Mumbai on line from 7th October to 8th October. Ravi told his father that he will reach Delhi on 7th by early morning Jet flight. Both father and son checked in Room No.401 on 7th. It was 8am in Delhi. Kavya called up Ravi to say that dad and mom would like to meet you all at 11am and you would have lunch with us after that. It was an unique fear. It was like appearing for your job interview or equal to going on a blind date.

As scheduled both Ravi and Veer Singh reached Vasant Vihar at 11am. Kavya was waiting along with her father Arvind Singh and Mom Santosh at their main gate. Both the parties greeted one another. Ravi was meeting her parents for the first time and Kavya's parents were also meeting Ravi and Veer Singh for the first time. Ravi's pics were already seen by them but Veer Singh saw the girl for the first time.

Veer Singh by nature was a very simple man, typical of a Jat. He did not have any specific preference because he knew that Ravi should marry or else no one would give him daughter after knowing their past. He, on the first glance, didn't find any reason of rejecting Kavya.

For him, Kavya was beautiful, fair complexioned, tall, big eyes attractive and an educated and cultured family. Incidentally Arvind Singh also happened to be from the same caste and culture from Rajasthan.

Both the parents discussed their roots. As it was not easy to leave your entire past life so Ravi informed them each and everything of his past including Pooja. He did not say anything about kids because he was not aware of. Kavya's parents were aware about his past because Kavya had already informed them with minute details. Both Arvind Singh and Santosh, were happy as Ravi did not give any false impressions. The only thing unusual was that Ravi drank 5 glasses of water in sheer nervousness. It was a sensitive relationship and both sides have to have a certain kind of attitude and Ravi adjusted to all whims and fancies of a new family. When Ravi told them that he would be going to join Microsoft at New York, it was a little disappointing but a pleasant surprise to all. Arvind Singhji supported him whole heartedly. It was decided to marry both Kavya & Ravi after a period of five years. In two years, Ravi would settle down in U.S. then Kavya would be joining him after resigning from DLF and will try new assignment in U.S. later.

Both the parents agreed and a new relationship was established between two families. They all had nice lunch and left for their hotel. Veer Singh left for Bhiwani and Ravi stayed back and asked Kavya to spend some quality time together in the evening and next day.

CHAPTER – 20

Kavya in Connaught Place with Ravi

Kavya reached Janpath Hotel at 5:45pm to meet Ravi. She was looking gorgeous and unique in a Royal blue Salwar Kameez with Pink combination and a designer colourful dupatta. She always wore trendy and stylish clothes as her smart appearance had the magic touch among people. She was growing up thinking that a prince charming, roams the skies and plains just waiting for that special moment to enter her life, snatch her away and take her to that wedded bliss. Ravi was all over her mind and now since she had approval from the competent authorities so Ravi was like anything taken for granted. She was behaving like Cinderella or Snow White.

She met him in his room. Ravi was on moon after seeing her. She was looking as sweet as Cinderella, black curls, dark deep eyes with long eye lashes and face filled with innocence and love. Ravi couldn't resist staring deep into her eyes and actually he grabbed her up in his arms and carried her off to the bed. She felt loved and adored for the first time after commitments. Kavya asked Ravi, "Is this your way of spending quality time? Yes, sort of, was Ravi reply but agreed to go out at Connaught Place, Palika Bazar and Ajmal Khan market for some shopping for Kavya. They had dinner in Shere-Punjab at Janpath and Ravi dropped her at her residence at Vasant Vihar.

Ravi requested Kavya to meet him next day if possible as he had to purchase some dresses for him to take to U.S. and also discuss details about his going abroad. She agreed and promised to meet him at 11:00am in his hotel only.

Kavya came at 11:15am, the next day. They both planned to do some shopping for Ravi. She was wearing Pakistani Salwar Kameez with bright embroidery. It was with majestic and wonderful pink colour and it was making her more attractive. Today even Ravi in his grey shirt, black trouser, black polished shoes, were making him more attractive and dashing. Ravi asked Kavya, why she was looking more beautiful and radiant? Is it love or dove? She very simply replied "I am a simple girl who hides a thousand feelings behind my happiest smile." She also continued, "No mischief, Ravi we have a planned agenda, we have to go to South extension to buy few jeans and shirts for you. This is going to be all my gifts to you. Atleast you will remember me there when my these shirts will touch your skin. Yes I will remember you and remember you more when your these jeans will touch my skin, Ravi replied. You can't improve and you always suggest something else like the concentration of Arjun when taking aim of fish eye in according to Mahabharat" Kavya told him.

They purchased the required stuff and had lunch at Hauz Khas and also had some cozy moments in one of the corners of the restaurant, designed for young couples. "It was a kind of day to share with someone you love" she said. "It was the kind of day to cuddle with you Kavya. I would always be longing for you" said Ravi. Ravi had a flight to Mumbai at 5pm so he dropped Kavya at home and heard Kavya saying "Normally I would have cried in bidding you goodbye, I might still do later but I would gladly see you off as it was the need of the hour. After all Ravi belonged to Kavya. She turned over and saw nothing. For a crazy minutes she feared that she might be loosing her grip on reality. He went away and disappeared in the cab to Delhi Airport.

CHAPTER – 21

Ravi leaves to join Microsoft U.S.

Finally after three weeks, Ravi joined the Microsoft office at TimesSquare, New York. The moment he entered M.S. Office, the first thing, he noticed was a beautifully decorated signboard which read –

"Our mission is to empower every person and every organization on the planet to achieve more."

The H.R. department conducted the familiarization round first by showing him a presentation of Microsoft, basically the company structure, board of directors, products, different offices in U.S. and worldwise. He was specifically apprised about his areas of design and development of structural engineering and sustainability of the environment.

He was taken around the campus which was not less than a big city. Beautiful buildings, with Glass façade, green lawn and trees all over. In fact he never ever saw such beautiful ambience in India including Millennium City at Gurgaon. He was taken to a building which was actually his workplace office. It read civil infrastructure and green building technology centre.

There again he noticed another eye opening message on a signboard which read –

> "Our goals are to minimize the impact of our operations and products, and to foster responsible environmental leadership."

Building a sustainable future, was the message for everyone at Microsoft be he a board of director or a small technicians. Ravi was briefed about the board of directors. Mr.Bill Gates was the brain and soul behind the establishments. He was also informed about Mr.Satya Nandella, CEO and was introduced to him in the staff café. His one sentence, he still remembered – "Here in Microsoft, you are first a Microsoftian then Indian so work your best and establish your identity. Next day, he was informed about various offices in U.S. and all major cities of world and about the products of Microsoft. The major products which were briefed to Ravi were APPS, LUMIA, MSN, OEM, OUTLOOK MICROSOFT, accessories, Skype and the endless, list continued.

Before he was left to his own department, a list of charities run by Mr.Bill Gates, was handed over to him for his knowledge and also to raise a feeling of being human at Microsoft. Now Ravi's role was for neutralizing the Carbon emissions of his company in addition to design and help constructing Microsoft offices all over with the materials used from Carbon reducing sources. He was the team who were committed to increasing their purchase of green power and making long term purchase agreements to power their facilities with renewable source of energy and plan to reduce the energy by 30 percent.

He made few friends who were accompanying him in and around the offices and canteens. He was enjoying the ambience including the taste of Indian food with so many Indians giving him the company.

He shared the entire information with Kavya and his parents. Kavya felt happy for him.

CHAPTER – 22

Pooja in her office and home after 10 years

Time took a leap of another ten years. Pooja was 35 years and kids were past 15, attending 10th Standard at St. Laurence Secondary School in Vancouver. This school was 100 percent subsidized by Bill Gate foundation and was one of the best in the city. Pooja's business was prospering and her reputation in the architecture milestones was already under creation of reckoning and standing on repute. She was being considered as one of the best architects by Govt. of Canada.

For the last so many years, Pooja had been single. She was free from all dramas of a relationship but there was something missing. She often thought about getting back out that air and find herself a man. She at times thought that she could transform herself from a hard working woman into a desirable lover and enjoy the beauty of her love life and also share the pleasure of the company of her partner.

She had been thinking about one man John lately. He had a sweet smile and a sexy Mexican accent. He was cute tall and thin with curly black hair and mustache. But it wasn't just his good looks and accent that charmed her. He was a genuinely nice guy, easy to talk to and a person to share her personal secrets. John was more sensitive to the situations. He never discussed kids as baggage to move to a relationship. He never discussed Ravi in front of her. He knew that she might feel hurt if John insisted upon doing away with memories of her past. In fact John gave her enough time to grieve over the loss of Ravi from her life. She had already gone through a traumatic experience and was still emotionally vulnerable so he took things slow and allowed her to set the pace of relationship and was prepared to face ups and downs of life as now. They both got to know each other.

Pooja had some unexplained fluctuations of mood. As a woman many times she wanted to seek out of his company as she was still battling feelings of guilt over dating other man. John was a matured man and he wanted to enter the relationship with patience and understanding. He always knew that he was getting into a situation that would require more tact and forethought than a normal relationship that too with Pooja who was young and had two toddlers from Ravi.

John was in a serious love affair with Pooja. He knew that Pooja needed attention, affection, appreciation and trust. He not only started loving Pooja endlessly but also her kids and the kids were quite comfortable with John. They used to call him John, not John uncle.

Pooja had a very challenging career, two school going children, extended family so she was in a situation no to decide to plunge in the relationship with John or be like that only. Many thoughts were floating in her confused mind but the thought of being tied down with the responsibility of her kids, put her off. She left the decision on her maternal uncle and Aunty and finally on Lord Krishna.

Rajendra Singh thought that how long would they survive to protect Pooja from the evils of this cruel society. The world is so cruel and she is so young with small children. So they decided and agreed for this alliance between Pooja and John. Pooja by nature or by the circumstances became religious and kept herself so occupied that these things became secondary, the priority was kids, her future and future of her kids.

But she was a human being, she also had her natural needs and desires. Sex was something which woman had and the man wanted. She was young so for her emotions needed to be both expressed and contained. Her uncle, aunty both knew Pooja's psychological needs and behavioural changes. They decided to call John and discuss their probable marriage proposals. They called John for dinner on coming Sunday. They both chose Sunday because both the kids had some birthday party of one of their friends in nearby building.

CHAPTER – 23

John meets the family

John came sharp at 8pm and was greeted by Mr. & Mrs. Singh. Pooja was in the kitchen. Mr.Rajendra Singh asked John whether he would like to have some beer or wine? I don't drink so a normal fresh lime sweet and sour with Soda would be fine or any fresh juice would be Ok. They were surprised to know about this habit. Pooja subsequently confirmed and gave that entire knowledge of vegan to her uncle and aunty which she acquired from John in Singapore.

The conversation was started by Mr.Singh by asking both of them whether they had trust on each other? Whether they loved each other? Whether John would accept Pooja along with the kids? Whether Pooja would feel at home with John with her children? All the questions were answered as if John was prepared after having done his homework earlier. He simply said, "I loved her the day she confessed and confided in me to reveal all her incidences of life. I would love to accept Pooja as wife like as is where is." I would love her and respect all her wishes. He also said that he was a genuine guy unlike these foreigners. I would like to marry her according to Hindu customs and would get it registered as per local laws.

Rajendra Singh then turned towards Pooja and wanted to know her opinion. Pooja said, "she loved John the way she loved Ravi. John was the best possible man to become her husband and more so, the father of her two children." She only had two small or big conditions which John had to accept or reject. John asked, what were those two big things or tests, I had to undergo?

Pooja – One, you will never want new sets of kids. Sam and Sim would be only our children.

Two, I would only agree once both my kids agreed and respected John as their father.

The first condition was immediately confirmed by John. The second one was to be confirmed by Pooja and Singhs after talking to the kids. Pooja informed John that she would revert latest by next Saturday.

They all had nice Indian dinner. Mrs.Singh specially prepared 'Sarson ka Saag' and 'Makki di Rotis' and 'Kheer' which John enjoyed to the fullest. He left. He was a very satisfied man. He started loving Pooja more after their this discussion. The only question, John asked Pooja, "Would Ravi's presence in person or in discussions make any difference to our lives? Pooja was prompt to reply in confidence and said that any person could say that they loved you, only a few would prove it. She further confirmed that she believed that show respect even to those people who didn't deserve it not as reflection of their character but reflection of yours. John, I think, I have clarified myself.

CHAPTER – 24

Pooja discusses with Children

Pooja called both Sam & Sim and told them that today they would have a serious discussion with Mamma. Both the kids, were 15 years, matured enough to have their independent views. Their exposure in the college had made them understand most of the things including relationship. The relationship was not limited only upto mother and children but otherwise also. They never in the past questioned their mother for any relationship but today they became serious, self-composed and prepared for any question, advice to and from their Mom. Sam asked Pooja – Mom "I could see some cryptic smile on your face and you seemed to be proceeding towards narcissism." What could be the reason behind this? He was supported by his younger sister (younger by 5 minutes only). Yes, Mumma would tell you something very important and confidential and would expect opinion from both of you which had to be well thought, without any fear or stress. You both had attained an age where, we could discuss anything under the Sun. She told them that she was considering of marriage very seriously. No, Mom, we were too small to have got married, said Sim, jokingly to Mom and he was just 5 minutes elder to me. Pooja said that she was not talking about you, stupids, she was talking about herself with John. It was a shock for both of them and they both wanted a time out for some time to think and tell Mom their views. Ok, said Pooja.

In the evening both the children sat very close to their mother with inquisitive eyes and fear in their hearts with a thought that they would never hurt their mother. They both had been watching their mother struggling with so many odds of life as a single mother and she had never complained for anything. She didn't hide anything from her kids including the identity of their biological father. She had narrated the entire sequence of events of her life, her journey from India to Canada.

The kids also never insisted of meeting Ravi as they never wanted their mother to become emotionally weak. Pooja reaffirmed that she would never marry John in case you both were not supporting. Sam and Sim, both spoke in chorus that Mom, we didn't have any issues because whatever decisions, you had taken in past were all justified and well thought so we both would support you on your relationship also. You had already discussed with our grandparents so we would always respect and abide by your decisions.

We only had few questions, "why Nanu, Nani committed suicide? Were they really so weak that they couldn't fight those illiterate idiots? Here in Canada and U.S. even a single lady takes on everybody who behaved nonsense. Mom, atleast you could have fought. You were 18 or 19 years then. No baby, that time was different. Both the kids lost their cool and continued in anger. What happened to that man called Ravi? Where and why did he disappear leaving you in lurch?

Mom, I would like to meet that bastard who left you Mom, when you needed him the most. His sister also said that bro - I would be with you then. That man must have settled down in life with some bitch. Pooja asked both of them to chill and told them not to pass any judgement without knowing the facts. He was not like that. Anyway Mom, we would not let him have peace and he also had to suffer as you have had. Pooja consoled both of them and hugged both of them like they were kids. Mom, we are with you for whatever decisions you and grandparents took. Pooja got their consent and now intended to marry John. John also met both the children but this time not like Uncle John but as John. The kids never called him Uncle John. They always called him John inspite of Pooja not approving it. John was comfortable in being called John, a friendly gesture which he always wanted with the children.

CHAPTER – 25

Pooja marries John

In India, specially north side, gone are the days when horses were used to carry the bridegroom to brides place while his friends used to dance like mad and throwing currency notes on him. Now a days people use very expensive cars decorated like bride itself. Rajendra Singh planned some beautiful cars for John to arrive at their place as groom.

Interestingly John wanted everything to follow Indian including customs, decorators, food, music and the dresses for him and the bride. The first thing he requested was that he would arrive on a horse. To get a horse in Canada for marriage, was a problem. Sam took the responsibility as one of his friends had a stud farm. He arranged a white house, nicely decorated from the country side and when the horse arrived, Pooja's aunt noticed that it was a male horse whereas the need for the occasion, was a white mare as per north Indian customs. Everybody had a good laugh including Sam and Sim as they never knew that it had to be a female horse. Anyway, even that was arranged within one hour.

The mare was sent to John's place. John had an Indian friend, who arranged a Manyavar Sherwani from Indian stores, light pink, embroidery all over, white chudidar and typical Meerut type shoes shining like silver foil. Turban, with Jaipur multicoloured one was becoming problem but somehow even that was made available from one shop called Utsav fashion. John was made a Pacca Indian Jat groom. In fact all his foreign friends wanted to witness Indian marriage celebrations so a special Indian event management company was flown from London. His friends were also promised by Rajendra Singh to conduct a mock Indian marriage on them provided they all brought either their wives or girlfriends. They all religiously followed the advice, brought groom and brides wears from Indian shops and it was difficult to even recognize, who the actual groom was?

When everything was ready, they all were advised to wait for their mock marriages to take place only after the real marriage of Pooja & John. In consultation with John and Rajendra Singh, it was also decided to conduct all the Hindu rituals in a day. The list included ROKA, RING CEREMONY, MEHENDI CEREMONY, WEDDING RITUALS, RECEPTION and BIDAI.

First event took place when John came with his friends and relatives as a Baarat. The Baarat consisted some 50 people both male and female all dressed up in colourful Indian dresses like Sherwani and Ghangra choli. The entire Baraat was giving an Indian look except the colour of their skin. They all were welcomed traditionally by doing Aarti and spraying the scented rose water. The groom in his attire was looking very handsome with a sword hanging across his waist.

Roka ceremony was conducted for a commitment from both the parties means from John's side and Rajendra Singh's side also. This was followed by Ring Ceremony, exchange of rings between John and Pooja. Rajendra Singh as father of Pooja applied Tilak on groom's forehead, sweets and gifts were exchanged between two families. John got lot of jewellery for Pooja so it was handed over to Pooja by him.

Sangeet Ceremony was conducted after this. There were songs and dances from Indian side and so was reciprocated by John's friends in form of English songs and dances. Mehendi Ceremony for John and party was given a slip as there was no time left for Mehendi to dry and those foreigners had reservations for its effect on their skin. All Baraatis and Gharaatis were served typical Indian food and lot of sweets. Both the kids that day were dressed like typical Indian youth. They were Samar and Simaran that day, no Sam and Sim but they were enjoying the moments to the best possible mood. They were enthusiastically watching their mother as a bride and were feeling proud. They were also helping their grand parents in making preparations for everything.

It was 7pm and it was time for the actual marriage. The marriage celebrations were conducted in a typical north Indian Hindu system. Vedic yagna ritual was essentially performed as core requirement of the system. The primary witness of a Hindu marriage is the fire, deity (or the sacred fire). The fire was lit. the ceremony was traditionally conducted entirely or atleast partially in Sanskrit by Hindus as the language of holy ceremonies. A translator was also requested to be present to help John understand before commitments.

Panigrahan ceremony means holding the hand, a symbol of their impending marital union and the groom announcing his acceptance and responsibility, was conducted. The seven bows were spoken, accepted by both groom and bride and they were committed by both of them in front of fire.

English translation of commitment –

"I take thy hand in mine,
Yearning for happiness,
I ask thee, to live with me
As thy husband till both of us
With age grow old.
This I am, that art thou,
The heavens I, the earth thou.

They were both officially declared husband and wife. Both the children congratulated them first. This was followed by reception of bride and groom and all the important people, the entire luminaries of the city, architects and engineers were present. A very nice spread of Indian and continental food was served. Mr.Rajendra Singh arranged everything so nicely and dutifully as probably Karan Pal, Pooja's father would not have done.

Next day, early morning was the time of Bidai. Both the parents of Pooja now made all arrangement and were exuberant till this moment arrived. Till now, they did not leave Pooja alone even for a day. It was a difficult task but like any parents, they did that also. Pooja for the first time after a very long time felt as if she had lost everything in world. She was weeping inconsolably. This was followed by Rajendra Singh, his wife and the children. Their daughter, their mother was taken away by John but that is what happens in India. For few days, the kids stayed with the grandparents.

Next day both Pooja and John came to meet Singhs and kids. They both planned to go to Las-Vegas for Honeymoon. As John was explaining his tour to Las-Vegas, Sam casually or jokingly asked John, "John, can we also join your

Honeymoon? Sim was also partner in crime so she also said can I also John?" John very coolly replied, "Get yourself a boyfriend and a girlfriend then you can come along." They both left for 15 days honeymoon to Vegas.

CHAPTER – 26

Ravi & Kavya in LDR

It's almost eight years Ravi and Kavya never met however there was not even one day or night, they didn't speak to each other. She waited for 5 years plus two years as agreed. One year, Ravi's mother died, second year due to death of Kavya's grandfather. Normally no big celebration takes place in the families where such tragedies take place. She was crossing 30 and family was feeling restless due to uncertainty of their marriage. The pressure on Kavya was also increasing from her parents and relatives.

Sometimes even she started thinking, Never get too attached to anyone unless they also feel the same thing about you, because one sided, expectations can mentally destroy you." or sometimes absolutely opposite like "Don't be disappointed when nobody stands with you. Chanakya rightly said, "I am thankful to those who left me because they taught me, I CAN DO IT ALONE, TRUST YOURSELF."

While she was struggling with her dissimilar thoughts, she got a call from Ravi, How are you Kavya? I, today early morning thought of talking to you in regards to our marriage.

So far due to some reasons, beyond my control, I have not been able to talk to you on our marriage date though we have been talking all the issues including maintaining our long distance relationship by talking dirty? I knew that uncle and aunty would be in tremendous pressure. I have applied for two months leave from Sept. to October this year. So you have almost six months. Please check with uncle and aunty whether it could be managed. Kavya said that she would check with them.

Kavya – Aren't you getting old for the marriage Ravi?

Ravi – A man and a horse never get old for marriage or union or Mating. But when I see you on Skype, you are becoming hotter day by day and if the trend continues, we can postpone marriage for another 20 years. you would be on top of the scale of beauty.

Kavya – You don't have to put so much of butter. I am agreeing to whatever you say.

Kavya also narrated what happened with her last night. She continued.

I was sleeping last night with a thought that it was the longest 96 months, I had ever spent without you. I was quite lonely. It was raining at sporadic intervals. I could hear those dreadful thunders after lightening. It was kind of moments to share with someone you love. It was a kind of day to cuddle with someone you always need. She said that you were 12000 miles away. That night I felt lonely and my bed as cold and damp as grave.

All of sudden I felt your presence on other side of my bed. I opened my eyes, saw nothing but I could feel a kind of warmth coming from the side, you were sleeping. For the rest of the moments, without any hesitation, I slid over into the blessed warm pocket of warmth and cozy comfort and felt fast a sleep at almost at once.

Exactly, the same thing happened with me and I felt that we wee sleeping together in U.S. He told Kavya, leave or no leave, job or no job, I would be with you in India. Kavya said that we were destined to be together and all things would be possible for us including this one. Till then, Kavya let your hands be rested behind your head and apply full concentration to have me inside you and your brain and think me and only me. I would be present with you on same bed every night. He also advised Kavya that distances did not matter for the deep bond, we had. I would call you tomorrow to check whether you had comforted my IN-LAWS. Bye and see you in the bed tonight, said Ravi which was replied like, "you are a beast and would remain a beast and now a dangerous beast after eight years." NO, if God had wanted us to be perfect (NO BEAST). He would have made us that way, was the parting reply from Ravi. The flame gathered momentum and the countdown started.

CHAPTER – 27

Pooja with John on Honeymoon

John chose Las-Vegas for their honeymoon. Las-Vegas is a magical place of an out of this world honeymoon. This outrageous action and fun packed place never sleeps. There is much to Las-Vegas than the Casinos and free drinks. They booked themselves in Four Seasons Hotel.

They also took a Cabana on rent and enjoyed the day at the pool. In the second half of day, close at the pool. In the second half of day, close to the evening, they took a short one hour Yoga class alongside the Dolphin at the Secret Garden and Dolphin Habitat in MIRAGE HOTEL. In the late evening, they moved around Las-Vegas all by themselves and enjoyed the beauty of the city and too many marvelous hotels. The temperature was 25^0C and it was more than pleasant. They visited almost all the womderful hotels like THE BELLAGIO, THE VENETIAN, RED ROCK CASINO RESORT and SPA. The MIRAGE HOTEL is the wonder in itself. They returned to their room at 11pm. They had their dinner on the road side mini food joints.

John was a good lover because he could see, hear smell taste and touch. Pooja had learnt to notice what she found pleasurable and what she didn't find pleasurable. She had learnt to communicate with her partner about her sensuality and her sexual likes and dislikes. If something drove John wild, she knew without John letting her know. If something drove Pooja wild, John knew without Pooja letting her know. They were inseparable even in the bed. John wanted her to melt in him. They were both relaxed and were enjoying their love making. Since they knew each other so well by now that there was no fear of performance anxiety.

After all in a passionate sexual encounter, they both felt like devouring each other. For Pooja, Lust was a normal healthy part of romantic relationship. She was starved for it for so long. In fact for both of them, these sexual encounters, produced a spiritual fusion between them as they loved each other so much. This intimacy of their's, opened flood gates, flow started which got converted into floods. They finally united in Body and Soul. Next day they enjoyed Grand Canyon helicopter ride and saw the city from birds eye view.

They returned to their kids and Rajendra Singh house after a week.

CHAPTER – 28

Kids grow and reach Secondary Standards

B oth Sim and Sam were 15 years now and would go to 11th Standard in the same school. Though it was the same school but there was a separate building in the same campus. Everything was different from their earlier school, the building, teachers, facilities and friends. Pooja and John wanted to speak to the kids and explain to them the basic difference between Primary and Secondary School life.

Pooja – John, I think, both the kids are more close to you than me. They both could confide in you so I would like you to speak to them and brief them as what all they are supposed to know or do over there.

John – It's quite natural Pooja because I call them Samar and Simranjit not Sam and Sim and they call me John, not John Uncle or Dad inspite your insisting every time.

Pooja – Yes, I agree and you are a good husband and a better father.

John – I will speak to them right away.

They all planned to go to a nearby restaurant for lunch and discuss with kids as an open chapter. John addressed them as Hi Guys, I would like to discuss your new school of 11ᵗʰ Standard. Are you aware of everything about your new school? No John, we have only seen the building, well, there can be no doubt that one of the major milestones in your life will be transition from 10ᵗʰ to 11ᵗʰ Standard. From childhood to adulthood, high school allows to gain a sense of what it will be like to become an adult. Whereas on the other hand, college allows you fully take ownership of your time, responsibilities and also who you want to become. As long as you are able to stay on track of the goal at hand i.e. getting marvelous grades, keeping a smart of schedule and studying like crazy, you will be just fine. The simple law in college, will be work a lot, have a little fun.

In school you know everyone in the class whereas in college, you will be lucky to know one person in your class with honesty and integrity. In school you have to live with your parents whereas in college, you get to live with your friends. In school, "you had the curfew, you had to follow, whereas in college you use your own judgment. This college will offer a variety of extracurricular activities for students to get involved. These activities are designed to enrich your student experience.

The stress level will be considerably high so to overcome this stress and to succeed in your studies, you will need to develop new friendships and improve your self esteem and confidence. You will need to show an increasing interest in school and school/college work. You will need to participate in all possible extracurricular activities. You will need to be practical and overcome emotions of the transition. You will also have a greed, desire to have some girlfriend or boyfriend but you will always remember your primary goal.

We will be the first persons to know about this, preferably me then Pooja. Do you both have any question? No, John, Thanks for a beautiful piece of advice. We will, but I will still call you John, no dad. Simaran might change her opinion. I will call him dad, said Sim. Pooja was very happy and confident of her relationship with John and thanked him. John Said, "I will take my rewards later in the night from you. Shut up, John, Pooja told him.

CHAPTER – 29

Ravi in Montreal

R avi was invited to address a meeting of all the member countries who had signed Montreal Protocol in Vancouver. In his opening remarks he said that too much of relaxations have been offered in this Protocol for replacing Ozone depleting substances (ODS) specially Hydro fluorocarbons(HFC) i.e 55 percent by 2010 and almost 100 percent by 2050.

Keeping the impact on environmental and our responsibility to the coming generation, we would not have such luxury of time and we will have to be free from ODS latest by 2040. This would be possible only and only when the Governments of all the countries including 108 signing countries keep this at their top agenda. India, China and Brazil would have to do much more than this.

The depletion of Ozone layer has already reached a dangerous level. Even though Montreal Protocol, has produced huge site benefits because many of the Ozone depleting substances/chemicals are more powerful heat trapping gases but all those benefits are now eroded by the rapid growth of Hydro fluorocarbons (HFC) and super greenhouse gases which are coming as substitutes for HFCs, are benefitting the humanity.

On behalf of his company, he also expressed his desire to trade Carbon Credits earned by his company to the benefit of poor countries to reduce their environmental liability.

Under the growing demand and rising prices, energy independence and impact of climate changes, building sector has become the primary consumer and all out efforts are to be made to decrease the natural energy consumption. This would only be possible by incorporating energy efficient strategies into design, construction and operation of new buildings and improving old buildings by energy efficient equipments.

He was emphasizing the need to reaching the concept of Net Zero Energy Building (NZEB) and also exploring Renewable Energy Systems.

Ravi thanked the audience and left to speak and encourage the students of St. Laurence Secondary School and junior college which was a wholly owned subsidary of Bill Gate Charity. He introduced himself, "I am Ravi Singh from MICROSOFT U.S. designing structures of the building and purpose of my visit to your school, is to make you people aware of your responsibilities towards the nature and environment." Could each one you, please introduce yourselves in short?

I am Samar Singh (SAM) born and bought up in Canada. My parents Pooja and John are the leading architects of Canada. I am Simranjit Singh (SIM) born and bought up in Canada. My parents Pooja and John are the leading architects of Canada. Subsequently every student introduced him or herself. These names rang a bell in Ravi's mind and heart but he concluded his address to the students as under.

Guys,

I will discuss with you about the power conservation. The Generation of power requires some fuel like diesel, petrol, steam or any other source of energy. To generate power, you all need this which in turn generates Carbon dioxide CO_2.

As the demand for energy around the world grows, it creates pollution and drives climate changes so becoming more energy efficient is the cheapest and fastest to cut energy bills and reduce carbon pollution. There is continuous improvement to help strengthen natural standards for heat pumps and create the first ever regional efficiency standards for air conditioning equipment and furnaces.

Ravi further told students that his company had worked with officials in China, India, Chili and Brazil to adopt strong energy efficiency policies. We are also helping India, China for wind power, solar power. Selection of building material like bricks, glasses, air-conditioning equipments and improving water quality also. We are helping them in devising new sources of energy like Geothermal and evaporating cooling process wherever possible. You all would be responsible citizens of this great country and would take the reigns from our generations.

Thank you very much for your time guys.

Everyone left the auditorium except Ravi, Sam and Sim. Sam asked, "Is Ravi a very common name in India Sir?

Ravi – Why do you ask this?

Sam – Because the name sounds as if me and my sister Sim have heard in the past.

Ravi – Are you both twin brother and sister?

Sim – Yes Sir

Ravi – Ravi is a common name in India. Is your mother Pooja from India or Srilanka?

Sam – She is from India and our father is from this land of Canada.

The kids thanked him and left for their house. Ravi also left for his hotel to take an early morning flight to New York, the next day. He was uneasy throughout, with the name Pooja and being architects, he became numb, restless and reached Grand Hyatt.

CHAPTER – 30

The Kids discuss Ravi with Parents

Both Pooja and John came home late but the kids were patiently and very inquisitively wanting to tell them regarding their meeting with one gentleman called Ravi. Over a hot cup of coffee, both Pooja and John heard them coolly.

Sam – Mumma, Today we met one man called Ravi from MICROSOFT U.S. He gave our school a very electrifying lecture on energy saving and caring the environment.

Pooja – So?

Sim – Nothing out of blue except when we told him that we are Sam and Sim, he did ask us to expand our names.

John – Ok, then what happened.

Sam – John, we also asked him, if his name Ravi is very common?

Pooja – Was he an engineer or a teacher?

Sam – I think, he was a teacher.

Sim – But he was talking about Solar Power, air-conditioning system, structural design of buildings.

John – Ok, he may be a nice guy. Both of you enjoyed his lecture or no?

Sam – Yes

John – What about you Sim.

Sim – I also liked it Dad.

The kids went away to their rooms. Both John and Pooja, were sitting alone. Pooja had that fear whether Ravi was same as that Ravi? John studied her serious mood and said, "Pooja, How about meeting that man?

Pooja – No John, why complicate your life for such petty issues.

John – You decide. I have no problem and even you have no problem. If you agree we can meet him in that Indian Restaurant Tandoor. Pooja seeing the trust and confidence in John eyes, agreed to meet him.

An hour later –

John and Pooja reached Tandoor and asked a table for four. Ravi arrived. Yes, it was same Ravi from the same rural background of western UP. There was no change in him except, he seemed a bit more sophisticated. John took the lead.

John – Hi Ravi, I am John and she is Pooja, my wife. I hope, both of you know each other.

Ravi – Yes, we come from the same background, same school. How are you Pooja?

Pooja – I am good, I have two kids, who met you, yesterday. John is my husband and a very well-known architect and town planner of this country. He is an famous in US & Singapore also. We have been married for almost one year now. You tell us something about you now.

Ravi – I am in US, working for MICROSOFT looking after Structural Engineering and green building aspects of the company buildings. I came here on invitation from Canada Government on Montreal Protocol and in the process, met you both and both your kids.

John was a matured man so he tried his best to ease out the conversation between Pooja and Ravi. Since he knew everything about Ravi and Pooja, so nothing mattered to them and in fact, he even asked Pooja, whether they would like to have some moments in isolation? Pooja said, No.

Ravi – Pooja, "Do you have any hate or ill feelings for me now?

Pooja – I don't carry any hate in my heart. If I loved you before, I have still got some sort of love for you." Just stay away from me though. My weak moment may empower my strong resolve and determination to survive even in adverse circumstances. I have John to take the responsibility of me and our kids. My kids would never know that the person, Ravi, they met, was actually their father because John is the real father for them and an ideal husband for me.

Pooja – John, let us have our dinner like an official dinner and close the chapter. Ravi left Tandoor, probably a happy man and John was a happier husband. He looked at Pooja, just hugged her and kissed her and said repeatedly that Pooja was a small crazy child stuck in a hot woman's body.

CHAPTER – 31

Ravi refuses marriage to Kavya

He couldn't sleep the whole night. His past and existing present was bothering him and he was mentally bankrupt. All his senses had stopped working. He had kids whom he couldn't call his own. Pooja was already happily married and he had no moral right even so speak to her. He boarded the first early morning flight to New York. All the young kids in flight were looking like his kids.

With guilt in his heart, he did not know what to do.

Another side was Kavya who endlessly waited for more than 10 years for his life partner Ravi. What was her fault? The only fault, she committed was that she loved Ravi selflessly. How would he face her? People say, "Love is blind but for him everything is dark and blind. He had grown up kids through not staying with him but now marrying Kavya was out of question more on moral grounds. How would he convey to her, this decision of not marrying her now? She was already 34 years and in fact waited 12 years for him.

Honest communication was the key to resolving relationship issues specially marriage. While she might hurt if Ravi didn't marry her. It was important to consider that marriage under present circumstances might mean something completely different to Kavya but please note that both of you couldn't have stayed in a relationship that didn't end in proper marriage and would fall apart as it was being made on the foundation of dishonesty and was far away from real love and truth. So he decided that it was better to end this relationship now.

We loved each other but..................... Love is not an emotion, it's a commitment.

Ravi allowed himself one more chance to think whether he would marry Kavya and would forget Pooja and her kids. He would die with these facts concealed in his heart without Kavya knowing them? He thought that when her relationship with Kavya was formed, all the factors like her charm, her hobbies, her interests, her personality and her openness were judged. She was vibrant, trusting and full of emotions. She still had all those assets which Ravi would never forget. For Ravi it was ignorance, he was innocent but this ignorance or Ravi's innocence would make Kavya life a living hell for which she was not responsible at all. She didn't deserve this. Ravi asked himself, "Do you want this person? Or do you not want to lose the relationship?" The greed in him said, "Yes, I do not want to lose either this person or the relationship with her." But his inner conscience said, "No, it was cheating, non-ethical and unpardonable sin." She lived to love you Ravi and no man loved her more than you loved. Ravi sunk into the depth of depression & defeatism. Then he understood that this was a frightening and overwhelming question to ask yourself Ravi. The voice from his heart came, "Ravi, build some courage to approach truth and tell Kavya that you will not marry her." He decided that the best, he could do was to talk to Kavya about what he felt and be open and honest with her and let it be evaluated by her.

Ravi called up Kavya and told her that he would be in Delhi for 10 days and would discuss something very urgent with her and her parents. He got 15 days leave sanctioned from his office starting next Friday onwards.

Kavya was all excited and happy to know that Ravi was coming but an unknown fear in her mind was doing the rounds. She had no option but to wait and watch. Ravi came to Delhi and called Kavya to meet him in Janpath. She came at 4pm. She was wearing a brown silk Salwar Kameez. He looked at her hair how it was falling down wildly into loose waves. She was looking more fresh which made her look even more glamorous than usual. Her dark black eyes glistened as the light from the Sunset hit them.

Ravi narrated the entire sequence of events right from his visit to Canada, his lecture at his kids school and subsequent meeting with Pooja and her husband John. Kavya very patiently listened to the entire episode. She had lots and lots of moments of weakness as it was absolutely normal to feel beaten, weak, helpless and of course numb and missing senses.

Ravi told Kavya that he had proved neither a good lover, nor a good father and he felt that he would not become even a good husband. He asked Kavya whether it would be appropriate to marry her under these circumstances. He is full of guilt for not knowing that he had two kids of grown up age and he had wasted the golden years of Kavya. Kavya did not utter even one word but certainly felt apathetic, gloomy and lonely, a feeling of cynicism. She was nearly slipping into clinical depression but she composed herself, gathered courage to listen and face the inevitable.

She eventually started understanding that a break up was almost certain. It was hard and finding her feet after break up is still harder. Getting up stronger was something, Kavya did herself and in the subconscious mind, she blamed Ravi also. Nothing rejuvenated her and made her normal. It is commonly thought that women get hurt more after a breakup but with time, they recover more fully than the men who lost long with the pains.

Kavya even if she never recovered, she composed herself and told Ravi, "Please discuss the same things with my parents, they would be more hurt but would understand you more that I have understood." Though they both loved each other to the core but they needed to be separated because of societal and geographical boundaries, expected unroyality to Kavya due to kids and Pooja being on the scene. Ravi requested Kavya to wash him right from her hair, throw on lipsticks and heels. Kavya asked him to come in the evening to meet her parents. Ravi agreed. He reached at Kavya's place at 9pm. Since the parents were briefed by Kavya, so no long explanation was required. They understood that Ravi genuinely was not aware of Pooja's marriage and the kids. However Ravi once again narrated everything in details. They only asked Ravi whether he would like to still marry Kavya? Ravi's reply without thinking much was that Uncle, I didn't feel comfortable and ethical in marrying Kavya, however if Kavya said, yes, then he would also seek your blessings and would marry Kavya as Kavya was one he loved, missed throughout. The parents asked Kavya, "For us nothing is as important as our daughter, we would always respect her feelings and also respect her wishes and her feelings." So Kavya you were to guide us beta. Kavya excused herself for half an hour till they all had some starters before the main dinner.

Two thoughts came to her mind.

1) Philosophically "Anything which belongs to you, will be somebody's tomorrow. Anything, you possess today, will be possessed by somebody tomorrow. Even the soul in your body doesn't belong to you, it will enter in some other body tomorrow. It is not something which Kavya says, it is written by him long long back."

2) Kavya decided to dump Ravi rather than she getting dumped. She realized and largely felt that she would be in position to release anxiety and separation chemical faster from her brains as Ravi would take months and years to get back to normal. She came out of the other room and joined everybody at the dining table and announced. Mummy Daddy, I had thought it over again and again and with your permission, I would like to tell Ravi, not to have any pressure, guilt from my side. He could take all decisions of his life without involving me. He was a free man and I do not have any hard feelings for Ravi. I would wish to be friends forever if it was Ok for Ravi.

Ravi replied, "I am not sure of anything or any future of my life but I will always be a friend to you Kavya." Ravi left their place with no curse either from Kavya or from her parents.

Ravi and Kavya never met since life has moved on but even after all these years, she still had a piece of his heart that skips a beat just for him and vice-versa.

Kavya always believed after this –

"Don't be disappointed when nobody stands with you.

Chanakya rightly said,

I am thankful to those who left me because they taught me, I can do it alone. Trust yourself."

CHAPTER – 32

John, Pooja a happy family

John had a very happy family. He was staying with his wife and two children who were in 3rd year of architecture course. They both were doing a great business and were a name, everybody knew in Canadian field of engineering and architectural achievements. They all had a very strong bond between all of them. They spent quality time together. All the family members were related by blood or by choice but their relationship was homogeneous to that extent that everyone thought that John was the biological father of Sam and Sim.

Sim who was very close to her father, once expressed the desire to see Europe during her vacations. John didn't even wink and think for a minute and booked a 14 days tour to Europe called "BEST OF EUROPE". After exams, they all set out for a planned tour of 14 days through the best of Canada's travel agency. They took an early morning flight and reached London, now the tour started. They were in a large group of 40 persons, men, ladies and kids. They were advised to strictly follow Rule 6, 7 and 8. It means you have to get up at

6am, get ready at 7am and be in the tourist bus after breakfast at 8am. Though the schedule was tight, not very suitable to the kids, but they all appreciated and respected it.

DAY 1 - ENGLAND

The city tour included visits to Tower Bridge, Buckingham Palace, Big Ben, Trafalgar Square, houses of Parliament, Prime ministers Downing sheet, Hyde Park and St. Paul's Cathedral. They were also taken to Madame Tussadd's Wax Museum to photograph yourself with world famous celebrities. All meals were arranged by Indian Restaurants duly planned by famous Indian Chef.

DAY 2 - ENGLAND-FRANCE

They enjoyed the Eurostar Travel from London to Paris. Visited Eiffel Tower top level to get a panoramic view of Paris. They took the Seine river cruise and the kids enjoyed this cruise experience to the fullest. After the meals, they enjoyed the magnificent view of Paris city by night which included Eiffel Tower, Champs Ely-Sees, Place de la Concorde etc. they returned to their hotel late night but again to follow the same rule of 6, 7 and 8.

DAY 3 - PARIS

It was wonderful experience at Euro Disney. They all experimented with various rides and shows like Honey-I-Shrunk the audience. They in the evening saw the famous Cabaret Show. Now the kids were grown up so it was Ok for the parents.

DAY 4 - BELGIUM, NETHERLANDS

It took them four hours by luxury bus to reach Brussels, went straight away for photostop at atomium. It was a long walk to visit Grand Place Town Hall, Statue of a little boy, John reminded Sam that he used to do something like this. Next stoppage was at Amsterdam city where they all enjoyed the city tour by Canal cruise.

DAY 5 - GERMANY, AMSTERDAM

They visited Tulip Garden. What beautiful gardens were there. Next stop was Mathurodam, a replica of Holland. From there, they all reached Cologne and next was a photostop at Cologne Cathedral. Sam and Sim felt that they needed atleast a month to follow this tour.

DAY 6 - COLOGNE-MUNICH

They arrived in Munich, the city for Olympic games many times, it was an orientation tour of the city which included HOFBRAUHAUS and the Opera House.

DAY 7 - MUNICH - INNSBRUCK

It was interesting and tempting to Pooja to visit SWAROVSKI crystal world. John gave her some nice diamond necklace. In the evening, it was a walking tour of INNSBRUCK including, INNS river, Golden roof etc.

DAY 8 - ITALY

Arrived at Venice, did city tour of Vaparetto Water, bus ride to Venice Island, bridge of Sighs Doge's Palace, Glass blowing factory and saw how they made a nice horse out of molten glass. They all took a romantic Gondola ride in the famous Canals of Venice.

DAY 9 - VENICE-FLORENCE-ROME

They proceeded to Rome by Bus and on the way visited Plazzale Michelangelo point and statue of David at Florence and reached Rome.

DAY 10 - ROME PISA-VALENZA

The city tour of Rome included TIBER river Roman Forum and photostop at Colosseum from outside only. It was a wonderful historical sight. Later proceeded to Pisa Tower. What a beautiful piece of architecture, standing and defying law of gravity. On way they saw square of miracles, cathedrals.

DAY 11 - VALENZA - LUCERNE

They after a long journey arrived at Lucerne in the evening.

DAY 12 - VALENZA – MT-TITLIS

This seemed to the most excited day as it included excursion to Engelberg. Mt. Titlis, experience on Titlis Rotair, the world's first revolving cable car ride to Mt. Titlis,

Thrilling ice flyer ride and snow sliding. In the evening, the tour included lion monument, wooden bridge. Some free time was given for shopping. They all were served dinner at lake Lucerne cruise with Swiss Folklore music.

DAY 13 - LUCERNE - JUNGFRAUJOCH

Another day full of pleasant and excitement was excursion to Jungfraujoch, top of Europe. We were all carried by a Cogwheel train from Lauterbrunnen to Europe's highest railway station i.e. JUNGFRAUJOCH. They all enjoyed the magnificent alpine scenery. Lot of snow clad mountains, ice skating was also enjoyed. They returned on the same train and later in the evening, they enjoyed orientation tour of Interlaken city and chocolate show followed by dinner. Sam told John that there were so many beautiful Indian girls, I was attracted to. John ADRIB replied, there wasn't even one close to your Mom when it came to compare in beauty with brains. Pooja simply blushed.

DAY 14 - LUCERNE GENEVA

They arrived at Geneva. Enjoyed Geneva lake and view the mount Blanc Jet d'Eau. It was the highest water fountain. They boarded the flight back to Canada.

John asked Sim, "what has been your experience?"

Sim – Dad, Germany is very beautiful country and Switzerland is superior to it. The tour was hectic but I enjoyed it thoroughly dad. Thank you so very much.

John – Anything, anytime for you darling and Big Boy – 'what are your special comments.'

Sam – More or less same what Sim had told you John. Indian girls are more beautiful than our white skinned blondes.

John – So?

Sam – So, nothing, I would marry someone like my Mom. She is the most beautiful woman on earth. John "You are lucky".

With this discussion, they reached home.

CHAPTER – 33

Happy Family continuation

One Sunday afternoon, John was sitting with Pooja at home. The kids had gone for a football match. He suggested to Pooja, "we have had no gettogether for a very long time due to Kid's exams and our trip to Europe so let us all sit together for a special dinner and chat on dinning table." In fact I was thinking for long that we four of us would have some formal and important discussions. Pooja said Ok, we would have it today evening only. What would you prefer for dinner John? John suggested full Indian meals with lot of spice and Kheer in particular.

Pooja said, "John, at one point of times, when I used ot make vegetables or chicken with spices, you, used to sarcastically pass comments like, "oh, that is the reason Indians need water next day morning to extinguish the fire of spices. Today you are asking for the same why? I have become 3/4th Indian in my eating habits" said John.

She prepared black Daal with lot of white butter, spicy lady fingers and chicken with lot of curry, typical Indian style.

She also prepared Kheer with milk, cashew nuts, Pistache. Everything was cooked as per John's likes.

They all set on the dining table. John had some Vodka with orange juice, kids had some white wine and some breezers. Pooja as usual, was sitting with her fresh lime water with Soda, Sweet and Sour. After the drinks, John addressed both the kids one by one.

John – Sam, now you are almost in the final year of your architecture course and you have to think about your future course of action, your job etc. I have to ask you a simple question, whether you would like to work in our company or do you want that I should start a new company for you?

Sam – John, I would like to continue the legacy of you and Mom.

John – That is perfectly all right for me and Pooja. What about you Sim?

Sim – I would also join your company dad.

John – What happens when you get married tomorrow and your hubby, happen to be from U.S. or India?

Sim – Dad, first of all. I am not thinking on these lines secondly if at all, it happens, my dad is so great, he will offer him also a job so that we all stay under this roof with Mom and dad.

John – I thought so and even I can't afford you to stay away from your dad. It is your turn Pooja. You are already established architect in and around Canada. Would you like me to open a branch in Mumbai or Delhi if you are slightly interested.

Pooja – I am better off here only and not interested in being connected to India again.

John – I knew that also. You all are so dear to my heart that I understand you before you express it.

They all enjoyed that sumptuous dinner and thanked Pooja for the dinner. The kids thanked Mom and John for a splendid evening. They all retired to their bedrooms.

Pooja was emotionally so charged up that she practically surrendered herself to John in totality and needless to say that both husband and wife felt as if they were on their honeymoon and it was the first day.

CHAPTER – 34

John goes to office but not Returns

Next day John had a lunch on meeting with top management team of Starwood Hotels and Resorts at Hyatt Hotel some 24 Kms away from his office at Ring Road. He got up early, prepared coffee for himself and got ready to move to his office and then to Hyatt Hotel. He wore a light grey suit, white shirt and dark blue tie. He chose to wear black polished shoes and white shocks. He was looking very handsome and dashing to face his clients. Pooja prepared some continental breakfast. Before leaving, he hugged Pooja lightly, gave her few light pecks on her cheeks and told her that Pooja was looking prettier than before. Pooja smiled and wished him all the best for his meeting. She followed him after sometime to meet him in the office in the afternoon.

John gave a presentation of the project, as star hotel univocally said that it was one of the best use of space with maximum facilities and its façade was one of the best in all Starwood properties. John was asked to wait for sometime to make them understand and take the decision. After half an hour, he was called in the boardroom and was congratulated by all present. He was appointed the architect for the project and was also informed that letter of intent will be issued in next one hour and detailed work order within next 7 working days. They all had lunch together and John left after thanking everyone.

Before leaving Hyatt Hotel, John called up Pooja and informed her about award of this project to them. Pooja was overjoyed and congratulated John and also informed him for a celebration in the evening. John knew the meaning of celebration so was a little more excited.

He took his car from the basement car park area and drove on to express way to reach his office as early as possible. He must be driving his car at a speed of max. 60 miles per hour. All of a sudden, he saw a truck approximately 100 meter away from his car on the opposite side track. The truck lost its control due to tyre burst. It was fast approaching John's car from opposite side after jumping the divider. John tried his best to take to the left as much as possible but there was continuous flow of traffic on his side of road. In a few moment that unexpected, unhappening thing happened, John had a head on collision with that truck. He didn't remember anything after that.

Some Samaritans with the help of local police admitted him in nearby St. Peter's Hospital. His wife was called and he was taken for an emergency operations. The doctors informed Pooja that John had a serious head injury and his rib cage is compressed badly. He was in the serious condition of recovery. They would be doing their best but you might not see him now as he was on Operation Theater.

The operation continued for 10 hours for straightening his ribs and stitching his head and skull which had multiple fractures. His X-ray and MRI and scanning were yet to be done after some time. He was unconscious. He was transferred to

ICU for further examination and tests. Pooja was allowed to see him only once and what she saw of John, was a totally covered body from head to toe.

All the necessary tests were conducted like X-ray, MRI and Scanners etc. and doctors observed that the injuries on his head were more than what they expected. They finally informed Pooja that John had only a few hours to live. If your children wanted to see him one last time, they needed to come as quickly as possible. We are dealing with only a few hours. They told Pooja that she could talk to him as he would be in position to speak to you for some time.

The moment John saw Pooja, God only knew, where he derived the strength to speak to Pooja, "Sweetheart, you are the most important person in the world to me. I won't leave you, I promise, If you don't see me, I am on the chair or in the hall or in the bathroom. I am always with you."

How would she survive? How would she manage without John? He had been such a splendid husband and father. Pooja assembled both the children, all in their early twenties. The kids closed the door to spend a little time with their father. John could utter only few words telling both of them how special they both were to him. He wanted to speak to their Mom. He requested the kids to send her in. "Pooja you have been a wonderful wife and mother and have stuck by me in all thick and thin of our life. I love you more now."

Pooja could control her tears and asked John "You promised me that you would never leave me, what happened to your promise. You know that I can't live without you" John said, "No Pooja, you are strength in yourself. Go back to your old days when you just started your life in Canada." Tears gushed from the eyes of both Pooja and John. Pooja left the room as she couldn't take it any more. John laid icy. John was no more only a body remained there.

The kids asked, "Mom How is daddy now?" After a long pause, Mom turned to them and said in a sad and chocked voice "your father would be leaving us soon, I knew it but so suddenly that I didn't have the chance to tell him goodbye and that I loved him one last time. Mom – "we are not prepared for this big one". John was cremated as per Indian Hindu rituals as he wanted it that way. Time doesn't wait for anybody or for anything.

Six months passed, Pooja took an additional responsibility of a father to the children and Managing Director of the company and she practically lost herself in work and in her two children but the memory of John was constantly haunting her and it was noticed by the kids that whenever Mom was alone, John was always in her mind and heart and she was missing him all the time.

The children spoke to her.

"Mom, Don't worry. We will take care of you like John took. We are only one year away to join your company. Though John was not our biological father, but he taught us the meaning of life, respect and value for relationship and a love to you. He would always remain present in all of us. John, you were and are a father to me also. Sim was always saying it but today I say it DIL SE, LOVE YOU DAD.

CHAPTER – 35

SAM calls up Ravi

S am with the help of Google and internet, traces the contact no. of Ravi at Microsoft USA.

Sam – "I don't know much about your relationship with my Mom Pooja but I thought of sharing some bad news with you Mr.Ravi Singh. My father John has expired in a car accident. My mom didn't ask me to inform you but I know our accidental relationship with you so I thought of informing you.

Ravi – "It is worst news to me. How is your mother now?"

Sam – She is coming to terms with reality but she might take some more time.

Ravi – I will see you all shortly.

Sam – Ok

Sam only informed Sim. Pooja was unaware of this.

Next day evening Ravi was at Pooja's place. When Pooja saw Ravi, she was shocked and surprised. She not even in her wildest dreams thought that Ravi would visit her to console her on her husband's death.

Ravi – "I am so sorry to hear about John. I met him once but I still remember, he was out of box and not a common man.

Pooja – Yes, but how did you know about John?

Ravi – Samar called up and informed me.

Pooja – Ok. He didn't tell me that.

Ravi – Anyway, Pooja, whatever has happened, can't be undone but if there is anything, I can do for you or for the family. It will be my pleasure and duty.

Pooja – Thanks Ravi, I will manage.

Ravi – Pooja, your silence is a sign of an emotional problem.

Pooja – There are people Sam & Sim with whom I can share "the real me" and during times of crisis I know whom I can lean for help and support. I was devastated when my husband died, but I know, I would get through it.

Ravi – Even then?

Pooja – Thanks Ravi for your kind words. I won't ever show my hurt, shame, fear, sadness or loneliness. I will be strong perhaps aggressive. I will be tough. I am a rock. I have been hurt many times before starting in childhood, when you left me, my parents committed suicide. I have made up my mind that I would never let anyone hurt me again. Thanks once again for your concern. You please take care of your family. If I need you, I will ask Sam to call you again. Bye, bye and all the best.

Ravi left Pooja but he didn't like that "couldn't careless attitude of Pooja. May be, she is too cheesed off.

Pooja called up Sam and fired him for having called Ravi without asking her. Maa, I thought he would provide you some solace as me and Sim couldn't see your this state of affairs.

CHAPTER – 36

Ravi back at Microsoft

This man, Ravi come back from Canada and got lost in steel, cement, concrete and trees. Ravi designed structure of a seven kilometer bridge over the American sea in such a way that steel required to support such massive structure was 50 percent as compared to the conventional design followed world over. He became a star overnight. His this design or this achievement was widely published in all daily newspapers over the world and it became a topic to read in all international engineering manuals, overnight he became a household name in Civil Engineers, Architects and Contractors.

This news even reached Kavya's doorstep via Hindustan Times, New Delhi with full details like E-mail, Twitter and company details with a small interview of Ravi's background, family status. In a single headline like HARYANAVI BOY, RAVI, MAKES HISTORY IN U.S. AND THE WORLD.

Some correspondent from Times Magazine asked, Ravi why he didn't marry? His simple answer was that he was already married with his work. He married to Engineering and had devoted his 15 years for such structure designs and she was his wife now since last 15 years. Yes, "He is happily married to his such dream."

"His personal pains, tragedy of life are far too small as compared to his efforts or his desire to do something for the welfare of humanity. Environment protection is one more dream, he has to be satisfied after doing something on it."

CHAPTER – 37

Kavya and her Milestones

Kavya completed 15 years of a successful and satisfying career in DLF, Delhi. Corporate office and she very proudly said that half of the commercial and residential buildings of her company in Gurgaon and Bangalore have been sold by her to the biggest corporates of the world including IT giants and hospitality barons. She was promoted as Vice-Presient, Sales and Marketing on Pan India basis.

This required a grand celebrations. Her company firmly believed that a company's greatest resource is its employees. Without them very little would be achieved. Kavya was considerably important as her contribution brought significant profit and raised the bar in reputation. That's why they celebrated simply to recognize and reward her to help maintain a culture of – motivation, unity and satisfaction.

DLF did it in style

1) They arranged a dinner party inviting who's who of Real Estate and hospitality industry of Delhi

including top Govt. officials and politicos. The company announced that Kavya deserved this honour as she along with her team wrapped up a two year project in just fourteen months. They all had exhausting weeks, full of tight schedule and deadlines. The entire gallery of people noticed her achievements and she became a star overnight.

2) DLF made a well-lighted neon board enlisting her achievements for public display.

3) DLF also issued a press note to highlight her milestones in all daily newspapers and magazines.

4) DLF announced a salary raise from Rs.60 Lacs per annum to Rs.90 Lacs per annum.

Kavya was happy and excited. She shared her this happiness with her parents and friends. Yes, she missed Ravi. He would have been more than satisfied but it didn't always happen what one wished. For Kavya, Ravi was still there in distant dreams. She confessed to herself that "She still wakes up with his name on her lips everyday morning. Yes, she is a simple person who hides thousand feelings behind that happy smile.

CHAPTER – 38

SAM & SIM
take total charge

Both Sam and Sim completed their studies and became certified architects. John would have wanted few years for them to work at some other companies but Pooja after the death of her husband, was at times, feeling uncomfortable in running the business, she was to hand over the reins of her business over to kids. She planned for family succession systematically. She very clearly told both her children that she was full time available to them for next 18 months after which she would devote her part time on as and when needed basis.

Since her children were interested and qualified to run the business someday, now was the time to begin establishing a strategy to implement a successful transition plan. Pooja introduced them to the key employees who were not family members. She introduced them to the financial advisor, legal advisor and the advisory board. They were given all information regarding Dos and Donts. They both started attending the office regularly with their Mom and also started attending all Client's meetings. They were nominated as Directors of the Company.

Pooja was not completely retired but she started exploring options as what to do next? Change is the rule of life. Fortunately, in most situation as one door closes, another opens. Pooja explored many options like CRY, HELPAGE etc. but she zeroed down to "HELP THE EARTH AS A SUSTAINABILITY CO-ORDINATOR."

She transferred all her architectural skill and project management skill to a career in sustainability. She joined a team of people who were knowledgeable, dedicated and principled. The entire team was deeply committed to protecting the environment. She was in constant touch with her team in different cities and countries like New York, Washington, Los-Angeles, Beijing. She became the youngest Non-Profit Volunteer.

Planning trees anywhere and everywhere became her pass time.

Meanwhile both Sam and Sim learnt the tricks of the trade and started establishing their own identity and growth of their business. Pooja was the proud mother of two professional business children.

CHAPTER – 39

Kavya at her place, Delhi

It was a Sunday. A day before, it was hot and sultry Saturday. July the 10th brought us a paradigm shift. Since morning Kavya was feeling the wind and rain in her face. Sitting in the balcony of her house, she was enjoying that torrential rains on the green grass of the ground in front of her house. Everyone was running here and there for shelter. The dark clouds were hovering all over with some frightening thunders. The weather was pleasantly cold turning chilly slowly. Streetlights were on even during day time due to dark clouds. In short, the weather was romantic and reminded Kavya her days at Mumbai where rains were always a sport for everyone. The sound of breeze mixed with rains, was providing a serenading effect.

Suddenly Kavya recollected her last meeting with Ravi at the airport lounge when both of them, had gone to a friend's marriage and college reunion. Kavya remembered each and every discussion regarding their jobs and places where they were working and where they were staying. Nothing was discussed regarding their families respectively. Neither Ravi told her anything nor Kavya did tell.

Last week, when she was going through Hindustan Times interview of Ravi, he said he was married to his work. Did this mean that the guy was still a bachelor or never married? This gave her a pleasant feeling. She started thinking with a concern and thought that he did not marry Pooja because Pooja was already married to John. What happened to his kids? With all these questions, remaining unanswered, she thought that she would explore all the mystery of universe of this man called Ravi and would bring the original Ravi back in him. She did it once earlier during her college days. She would do it again. She even thought that she felt so good sometimes to just sit by herself relax and not talk to anyone. But Ravi had control on her mind and heart.

She called up Ravi and this is how the conversation went between them.

Kavya – Hi, Ravi, Kavya this side. How are you doing?

Ravi – Hi, what a pleasant surprise? How are you Kavya? Where did you get my number from?

Kavya – I am good too. It's not difficult to get your number now as you are a celebrity of universe. Times Magazine is the testimony for this.

Ravi – Don't be sarcastic please. For you, I am same Ravi. You are no less.

Rajiv spoke to me and told me about all the glory, you got from DLF.

He told me that Kavya was looking larger than her size in all the newspapers. DLF was looking like a dwarf in description about the achievements and milestones, you have achieved. I feel too proud.

Kavya – So you are aware of all that? Ok, why you didn't marry. Did Pooja ask you to fuck off or what?

Ravi – She was already married even before I met her. I think I have told you about.

Kavya – Ok. Yes, you told me about it. What's future of your children?

Ravi – Both Samar and Simranjit are the pillars of strength and reason to live for Pooja so they are her children and I think, I will never ever have the right or moral to call them my kids.

Kavya – Ok. Now what is your plan of life?

Ravi – I do not know, Kavya.

Kavya – You were a Lalloo (stupid) then and you are a Lalloo now. Normally a male takes the lead but I think, in your case, I will have to do that role.

Ravi – Yes, would you do that? Or you are simply having fun?

Kavya – You don't have to stop having fun when you get old because you get old when you stop having fun. Grow up Ravi. When we were in IIT-B, it was a puppy love. In these years, when we were away, it was a Bollywood love. Now atleast when we are 40, let's have some matured love.

Ravi – Go on Kavya.

Kavya – On some serious note, Ravi, it's ok to move on from the past and the person that hurt you. Don't block your happiness, you can't let go of the pain.

It's Ok to fall in love again as advised by some expert in the past as under.

"It's Ok to fall in love again. Learn from all you have been through, we can't be so hung up on a situation, that didn't work, that we can end up missing, out on a potential blessings."

Ravi, allow yourself to feel real in you again.

Ravi – You sound genius. When I first met you, it was electric and it was easy. I wanted to be around you all the time. Next was a stage when we both couldn't keep our hands off each other. But times goes on, we had our first separation, it was quite normal. Now I can't afford to lose any of the luster from our relationship.

Kavya – Now you come to right point. Now listen to what I tell you for the last time.

We have already played a lot of hide and seek with our lives. Now the time has come, we have to end this game and find each other for each other. Can we be onesome in two bodies?

Ravi – Have you given me any option? But I like your not giving me any option. I have found my love again. I agree with you that it's Ok to fall in love again. Convey my butterful regards to uncle and aunty. I will meet you shortly to live with you till our last breath. Kavya, I love you forever.

CHAPTER – 40

The ultimate to happen

U ncle, Aunty. Please bless us. We would like to become
husband and wife. We do not want a big show. We will
have a registered marriage and host a small reception for all
the guests of DLF and associated contacts.

The registered marriage took place and a good reception
was arranged at Taj Palace, New Delhi. They both had gone
to NAINITAL for their honeymoon.

After a month, they both left for New York. MICROSOFT
very gracefully agreed to include Kavya also as their Senior
Manager.

Printed in the United States
By Bookmasters